NEVER DATE YOUR BEST FRIEND

NEVER DATE YOUR BEST FRIEND

USA TODAY BESTSELLING AUTHOR

JULES BARNARD

Chapter One

Nessa

I'm stuck in the friend zone. Again. What is it with me and guys?

I unload drinks from my cocktail tray, stealing glances at Zach and that woman.

The same blonde comes into Blue Casino every month like clockwork. She's beautiful, with short platinum hair tucked behind her ear in an overgrown pixie. Tonight she's wearing stilettos and a skintight black micromini dress. It's hard to tell, with the invention of Botox and fillers, but she seems older than Zach. Maybe mid-thirties.

Bartender Jimmy, in the sports bar where I work evenings, shakes his head. "Doesn't deserve you, girlie."

"What?" I shove the last empty glass to him. "I just find it fascinating."

Blondie hands Zach a plastic keycard. He stares at it, then glances up.

Right at me, because I'm looking. Again.

Our gazes lock, and for an instant, guilt flashes across his face.

I swivel my head toward the bar, my hands shaking. *Crappers.*

"Sure you find it fascinating." Jimmy chuckles, wiping the counter.

Pretty sure everyone suspects I have a crush on Zach Elliott. Except Zach. Or maybe he knows and doesn't care. Zach is my buddy—my buddy I want to make babies with.

I sigh and pinch my eyes closed, fighting the frustration I've lived with for more than a year. Zach takes special care to make sure we're *only* friends. It's humiliating. I pine while he passively rejects me.

The woman he's standing with walks off, and he flashes his hands to the cameras in the ceiling to show the house he hasn't any cards or cash tucked up his sleeve. He prepares to leave his blackjack table. To follow *her*. Like he does *every freaking month.*

Why her? Why not me?

The worst part is that Blondie isn't even Zach's only conquest. He hooks up all the time. I usually don't see him in action, thank God, but I hear about the women leaving his house at all hours. He flirts with everyone. Except me.

I slam my tray on the counter, and Jimmy lifts a brow. "Sorry," I mumble.

Keep it together, Nessa. I can't let it get to me anymore. I'm not acting like myself, and that's just messed up.

Jimmy's right. Zach doesn't deserve my heart. Only, I know him. He's sweet and funny, and wonderful. There are jerks who only care about hooking up and who treat women like dirt, but that's not Zach... though his behavior isn't exactly glowing right now, as he prepares to meet with Blondie.

I press my hand to the center of my chest. Hurts so badly. Why do I do this to myself?

I need to take a page from Zach's handbook. I should get out there and date. I won't do casual sex. Been there. The one-night stand during my senior year of college left me so empty it put me off dating for a long time. But I've been obsessing over Zach for a year and half, ever since I graduated from San Francisco State with a useless communications degree and moved to Lake Tahoe with a friend.

My friend moved on. I haven't.

Zach was one of the first people I met when I arrived, and initially, I felt this spark between us. I'd catch him eyeing me *that way*—with heat and longing—right before he'd wash the expression from his face and call me by some juvenile nickname.

He treats me like his little sister, and it's enough to make me lose my mind. I'm ready to pull my hair out. Which wouldn't be a good look. My long black hair hits my waist, and it's my best feature. Something is holding Zach back, and I'm tired of running up against that wall. The best thing for me would be to move on and stop daydreaming about what will never be.

I deliver a tray of new drinks, and out of bad habit, look for the person who's driving me bizonkers.

Zach still isn't at his blackjack station. And unfortunately, I know what that means.

My stomach cramps, my elbows pressing my sides. The movement tips my tray and the napkins resting on top tumble to the ground.

"Need a hand, Ness?" I look up into Sal's bright blue eyes.

Sal is a local who comes in to catch whatever sports

teams are playing on the big screens. He and a group of regulars meet up every week. Sometimes twice a week.

I hunch over, gathering the napkins. "I've got it, Sal. Thanks."

"Everything okay?" His expression is warm, concerned, as if he sees something in my face that has him worried.

Sal's a good guy, and he isn't bad looking. He's about my age, with killer blue eyes, tanned skin, and sandy blond hair. Unfortunately, he takes Tahoe Bum to a new level with frayed jeans where the hems drag on the ground, and his T-shirts are so thin from wear that they're almost see-through. But those things aren't why I can't see myself with him.

I can't see myself with anyone except Zach. And that needs to change.

"Yeah, just a crappy night." I toss the napkins on my tray and stand.

Sal wraps his arm around my shoulders. "Grab a drink with us tonight, Ness. We're heading to Farley's in a bit."

Farley's is a hole in the wall a couple of streets over. The indoor Cornhole game is a big draw among the locals.

I never take up offers from men who hit on me at Blue, which happens often, given my uniform. A sequined bustier and satin hot pants will do that to a girl. But Sal and his friends are laid-back. They seem more concerned with the beer left in their longnecks than the pretty women who pass through. They're not looking to fulfill their sexy waitress fantasies.

Sal's gaze drifts up and holds. I look over to see my friend Mira walking in, which explains why even Sal's head turned. He may be laid-back, but he *is* a male.

Mira is insanely beautiful. A man would have to be dead not to notice her. Too bad she's taken. She's in a serious relationship with my friend's brother, Tyler. Mira is what you'd call feisty. No one thought a guy could reach past the feist and find her soft core, but Tyler proved up to the challenge. They seem really happy together. And I'm not jealous that all my friends have suddenly settled down. Not at all.

Okay, a little.

Mira's gaze skims the people in the bar, searching. I wave her over.

Sal smiles at me. "Let me know if you want to come," he says, and turns to his friends.

"Hey." Mira drops her cell phone in her purse. She must have just gotten off work. "I'm checking to see if things are still on for tacos tomorrow night."

"Aren't they always?" Zach hosts a taco dinner every Wednesday at his place. It was one of the first things he invited me to.

I ball up the napkins that fell, which are useless now that they've touched the ground.

"Everything okay?"

"Yeah." I smile weakly. "I'm just in a pissy mood."

Mira's face scrunches in confusion.

Okay, so I'm not usually cranky. Still, a girl has a right to be in a bad mood every once in a while. Maybe I'll take Sal up on his offer. I could use a change of scenery. Watching Zach leave with that woman grated on my nerves.

I step to the side and pull Mira with me. "I'll cheer up. I'm just having one of those days. Sal invited me for drinks after work to blow off some steam."

Mira sizes up Sal over my shoulder. She had a tough upbringing, born into a drunken, drug-addicted home. She's overcome a lot, which has made her a really good judge of shady characters. "Cute, but..."

"I know. He could use a makeover. It's not like that, though. Sal's a regular. We're friends."

"Still, you want me to tag along?"

"Nah, I'll be fine."

Mira squeezes my arm lightly. "Nessa, are you really okay?"

I haven't outright told anyone about my crush on Zach, though they may suspect something. We're all friends, and talking about my true feelings could make things awkward.

"I'm fine. I'll see you tomorrow at Zach's?"

"Yup. I even made cookies for dessert."

"Holy cow—" I reach up and press the back of my hand to her forehead. "Do you have a fever or something?"

Mira laughs. "No. Tyler and I were in the mood for cookie dough last night. We ate half a container and only stopped when our stomachs rebelled. I made cookies with the rest of it."

"So this is store-bought cookie dough?"

She makes a funny sound in the back of her throat. "Of course."

"*Phew*, you had me worried there for a moment."

Mira chuckles and walks away. "I've been cooking lately," she says over her shoulder. "Look out, I've turned domestic. The next taco dinner may be at my place."

Oh boy. Zach is the only person in our small group of friends who can cook. Mira at the stove is a scary prospect. Her new position as an assistant to a top executive at Blue is perfect for her. She loves bossing people around in HR. But cooking? She's never cooked for anyone, as far as I know. Maybe she's been experimenting on Tyler. If so, the poor guy has been taking one for the team.

I walk over to Sal and nudge his arm with my elbow. "Hey there, I think I will join you guys tonight."

"That's my girl." Sal grins.

"I get off at midnight, so in about an hour. Does that work?"

"Of course. The guys might head over early, but I'll stick around and wait for you." He nods to the television screens. "They're about to show sports highlights again."

I wrap up my shift and mentally prepare to block Zach from my mind for an evening—longer, if I can stick to my convictions and move on.

Forgetting there could ever be an *us*.

Chapter Two

Zach

"There's my handsome."

Alexis is sitting on the bed with a glass of bloodred wine in her hand when I step inside her room after using the keycard she gave me. Her suite is top-of-the-line Blue with a full bar, views of the mountains and lake—no expense spared.

She walks over and grabs my ass, reaching up to plant a kiss on my mouth. I turn my head at the last second and her kiss lands on my cheek.

Her mouth pulls into a kittenish pout that's not the least bit attractive.

I step farther into the room, mostly to put space between us. "Why are you in town?"

"Can't a lady visit her favorite boy?"

The muscles in my shoulders bunch. "Man. I'm a man now, Alexis."

Her eyes glint. "Yes, you are." She walks up to me and palms my dick.

Funny. Even my dick knows when to run and hide.

I inch to the side, out of her grasp. "Look, Alexis, I've got things going on tonight. I can't visit with you." Not true, but I don't want to be here.

When Alexis cornered me at my blackjack table downstairs and publicly handed me her keycard, I was pissed. We've always kept our relationship quiet. But instead of looking around at the pit boss, or anyone else who might object to my fraternizing with patrons of the casino, my first instinct was to check the sports bar where Nessa works.

Nessa was already peering my way. Her eyes immediately darted to the side, but I thought she might have caught the exchange. I had the furious urge to snap Alexis's keycard in half.

"Darling." Alexis saunters to the chrome and glass dining table, and sets her wineglass down. "You look tired. You've had a long day at work. Take off your shoes. Hop in the bathroom for a steam shower. You'll feel much better afterward."

"No, thanks. I'm gonna head home."

Alexis was there for me after my mom's accident, eight years ago, and I have a hard time ditching her. I feel obligated where she's concerned. But that obligation is getting more and more difficult to stomach lately. I turn to leave.

"Zach," Alexis says. "Is everything okay?" She walks over, her expression soft. But I know better. Alexis's heart is impenetrable. She cares for me in her way, but I no longer find it genuine. In fact, I wonder if it was ever real, or merely formed out of selfishness on her part.

"Everything's fine. I'm just tired." *Mentally more than physically.*

She reaches for the buttons on my shirt.

"Stop." I push her hands aside.

My response isn't greeted with a kitten pout this time, but a look of genuine frustration. "What is your problem? I've always taken care of you. Ever since your mother... Well, for years. I'm the one who's been there for you, and this is how you treat me?" She drops her hands and turns her back to me, staring out the broad window overlooking my hometown.

I sigh. Alexis knows exactly how to make me feel guilty. Her actions may be based on selfishness, but she's right. She was my mom's best friend, and in some twisted way, she's been like a mother figure to me.

A mother I fuck. Jesus, that's messed up.

"I don't mean to be disrespectful." And now I feel like a jerk. But Alexis pushes too hard sometimes, and I'm not into it. I haven't been for years. I'd rather be friends. What we've been doing—it's wrong.

Alexis and I have been lovers since I was sixteen and she was thirty. She made me swear not to tell anyone, claiming they wouldn't understand. I knew she could get into trouble for dating me. I had no problem lying to everyone, as long as I kept receiving her attention.

I'm twenty-four now, and I know better. My reasons for keeping our relationship a secret have nothing to do with protecting Alexis from the law. I don't want people to know about us, because I'm ashamed. But this thing has been going on for so long that I don't know how to stop it. The few times I've tried, she's thrown a fit. Just like she's doing right now.

"*Zach,* you're not even paying attention! What is wrong with you? Stop fighting this." She reaches for the buttons of my shirt again, and I let her unfasten them. "You'll feel much better after a shower. And then, who knows?" She looks up and smiles suggestively.

I place my hand over hers and hold it to my chest, forcing her to stop. "I'll take a shower, then I'm leaving. Nothing more, Alexis. I'm not interested."

She steps back. "Of course." She walks to her glass of wine and takes a sip. "Take your time. I want you happy and comfortable in my home."

I shake my head. "This is a hotel suite, not your home."

She waves me off and moves to a chaise. "Same difference. Now hurry along. Your shower awaits."

I step into the bathroom and close the door, undressing as quickly as I can. I could use a shower, but I'd rather have one at my place. Alexis gets nasty when I don't do what she says. Better to appease her and take the damn shower than deal with her bitching.

But I'm not fucking her. Not in the mood—can't remember the last time I was in the mood. Doesn't mean I didn't do it, though. I'm as much to blame for this thing as she is.

I turn on the shower nozzle and don't bother with the steam. I'll be in and out, no frills. Just long enough to let her feel like she's taking care of me, and to get her off my back.

Scrubbing my head and body with the shampoo the hotel provides, I close my eyes to keep the suds out—and sense a shift in the air, as if the bathroom door has opened.

Fuck. I should have locked it. Alexis doesn't know the meaning of boundaries.

I don't say anything, though. Maybe she only came in to grab something, but I highly doubt it.

The *swish* of the glass shower door opening tells me I'm right.

Alexis stands in front of it, her arms crossed, ogling me. "Mmmm, you look tasty. Have you been going to the gym?"

I rinse out the shampoo, and turn off the water. "You

know I go to the gym. Mind handing me a towel?" She's blocking my exit, and beginning to piss me off.

Alexis stares at my dick, which is still dormant. No movement. None. And I can tell by the look on her face she'd like to do something about that.

"The towel, Alexis."

She rolls her eyes and hands it to me, stepping out of the way just enough for me to get past her while still grazing her body.

I ignore her presence and dress quickly. "Thanks for the shower. I better get going."

Alexis follows me out of the bathroom. "That's all? You're really not going to stay? Zach, you know I can take care of you and help you relax." She smiles and glances at my crotch.

I don't want what we've had anymore. And it's never been more apparent than tonight, with Nessa seeing me and Alexis together, and how dirty I feel right now. But I need to tell Alexis it's over someplace else, someplace where I'm on equal footing. Not inside this damn suite that makes me feel weak and filthy, and reminds me of every time we've ever been together.

"Not tonight."

* * *

The first thing I see when I exit the elevator after leaving Alexis's hotel room is Nessa walking up to some dude wearing a Chargers cap and flip-flops. Nessa's in tight black jeans that mold to her perfect curves, and a long-sleeved tee, a sweatshirt tucked in the crook of her arm. It's the end of spring, beginning of summer, and warm during the day, but the nights are still chilly.

"All set?" I hear the guy ask her as I near.

Nessa looks up and our gazes lock. At first she appears surprised, then her smooth throat bobs in a swallow, eyes flittering away for a second. She looks back and gives me a tight smile.

My gut knots. For a moment, I wonder if she knows where I came from. Or more importantly, who. But no one knows about me and Alexis, not even my best friends. Nessa did see Alexis hand me the keycard, which was damning...

Panic tightens my chest. No fucking way I want my friends aware of the truth, and especially not Nessa.

As I skim her pretty face to read what she may or may not be thinking, I notice again the guy standing next to her. Stifling the urge to reach for her and jerk her to my side, I say, "What's up?"

She introduces me to her friend, and I barely register his name. I'm too busy tracking the subtle flicker of her dark brown eyes, the tightening of her mouth. She won't look at me.

"Sal and I were just leaving for Farley's." Her voice is flat, cold. And totally not like her.

Even if she suspects something with Alexis, why the cold shoulder? Nessa knows I date around. And who is this guy, really? She's not starting to see him, is she? Things have been great with Nessa hanging out with my friends and me. Why does she need this guy?

"Wait up," I say. "I'll join you."

Her friend seems okay with me inviting myself, or else he's hiding it with a good poker face. But Nessa's gaze narrows, finally taking me in. I ignore the flare of anger I see there. She's more pissed than the dude I cock-blocked, and I honestly don't give a shit. Nessa is pint-sized, and I don't know this guy. No way am I letting her walk out the door with him.

I pull her to the side before she can refuse me. "I don't think you should leave with him."

"Sal's harmless."

"No guy is harmless."

"Some guys are. You're harmless."

"Not even me."

Her head notches back. I hadn't planned on saying that, but it's true. Given how messed up my life is, I've never been a safe guy for Nessa. Which is why I make sure we're friends and nothing more.

She seems to shake off my words. "Fine, whatever—let's go."

We walk through the crowd on the strip and make our way to Farley's. The place is packed when we enter, but the group Nessa and Sal are meeting up with quickly flags us down and buys a round of shots. I take that moment to let the tension from my run-in with Alexis roll off my shoulders. I need to do something about her. End it once and for all.

I get the next round of drinks, and we line up at the indoor Cornhole. *Best name ever.*

Sal—I'm reminded when I call him by the wrong name—hands Nessa and me four small sandbags. "You're up, Ness. Let's see whatcha got."

His familiarity with her grates on me. Who the hell *is* he? Seems like a typical Tahoe clinger. Why would she be interested in him?

Nessa sets her drink on the table beside us and lines up a shot, eyeballing the illuminated neon-green hole. The rest of the court is decorated with dusty holiday lights.

She tosses the sandbag into the air and it falls short, straddling the edge of the box.

"Little low there, Pipsqueak," I say, a smile in my voice.

Nessa's shoulders stiffen, and she glares at me.

I raise a brow at her. "Doth my presence irritate?" She faces forward again.

Hmm, a little touchy tonight.

I step up to take my shot. Nessa's on Sal's team. I guess because she's with him. Not *with him*-with him, but you know, she came here with him. And me—she came with me too. Okay, I invited myself.

Jesus, I hope she's not thinking of dating this guy. I've gotten used to not having to worry about Nessa. As a brother—worried like a brother would be. And if I have a strong attraction to the sweet, gorgeous brunette who hangs out with me and my friends, that's my secret.

I better at least get it on the board after I razzed Nessa for her shot. I let the sandbag fly and it lands on the edge of the hole.

Our teammates take their turns and we're even by the end of the round.

Nessa's up, and this time, she slides the bag home, her petite, curvy hips doing a little swish in victory.

She turns and smiles. "Sorry, didn't I mention I was a pitcher in high school?" Her partner walks over to congratulate her, and she high-fives him.

Damn, what's going on with her tonight? "Didn't know you played softball," I say when she returns to my side. "How long?"

"Six years. I played in junior high as well."

"Hmm. Interesting."

"Is it?"

"Kind of. What other talents are you hiding?"

Her light olive complexion turns rosy. "Nothing you're ever going to know about."

"Ouch," I say, but immediately my mind wanders. To topics I try not to think about when it comes to this girl. It damn well isn't easy, because just looking at her has me thinking of... things... hot, sweaty, naked things. With my things inside her things, my mouth on... *Stop!*

Time for a subject change. "What's up, Ness? You seem angry tonight."

She looks away, staring ahead as she answers. "Why were you coming from the Blue hotel elevators earlier, Zach?"

Which really isn't an answer, but a question.

My chest burns, and I feel my face flaming—not in embarrassment, but anger. With myself, for continuing something I should have put a stop to years ago.

"Does it matter?"

She looks me square in the eye. "Yes."

Hurt and sorrow fill her eyes—as if she knows what I'm not saying. Knows what I've hidden from everyone. It shocks and undoes me.

She *can't* know.

"I'm up." I avoid her question, because I don't want to tell her the truth, but I won't lie to her either.

I prepare for my toss. The guys on the other side are chatting and drinking their beers. They don't seem to mind that we've stopped in mid-game to talk about something I have every intention of avoiding.

"Who is she, Zach?" Nessa persists. "Why does she come every month? Why do you go with her?" Nessa's voice is soft, pained.

I swallow hard. *Fuck.* I'm not hiding anything. And why is Nessa so upset by it?

It's one thing for me to be unhappy with my arrangement with Alexis. It's another to see Nessa hurt by it.

"She's no one, Pipsqueak."

"Stop calling me that!"

The discussion across from us halts. The guys stare at Nessa. I do too, taking in the heaving of her chest, the flare in her eyes. *Whoa.* Never seen Nessa like this before.

I grab the sandbags from her hands and set them on the table, pulling her to the side. "What's up?"

She looks away. "I hate that nickname."

"Got it. No more Pip—" She shoots me a glare. "No more using that nickname. But I don't get what the big deal is."

"The big deal is that you treat me like a child. I'm an adult—only a year and a half younger than you. We're friends, but you don't need to rub in the fact that you don't see me as a woman."

What's she talking about? "I know you're a woman." God, do I know. I try to forget it every single day.

Nessa deserves a better dude than me. Someone better than the guys she's hanging with tonight too.

She tucks her long, dark hair behind her ear, the floral and orange scent she wears wafting over, sending my senses into overdrive. "I know you have something going on with her. There's something not right about it... but I'm done trying to figure you out."

My head pounds. That last shot is messing with my ability to think clearly.

I'm not hiding this from anyone. Or maybe Nessa is the only person perceptive enough to have figured it out.

I'm ashamed, but mostly the fact that Nessa has puzzled out the truth is a game changer. I can't do it anymore—can't stand the idea that my sordid relationship with Alexis is hurting Nessa. I was already going to end it, but I want it over this minute. I wish I had told Alexis before I left the hotel room instead of waiting to do it somewhere else.

Sal walks up. He glances from me to Nessa, a concerned look on his face before he smiles at her. "Hey, why don't we take a break? Can I get you another drink? What about you, Zach?"

"Yeah, thanks." I let out a sigh and inch closer to Nessa.

I'm not worried about her with these guys. They seem decent, and they haven't driven hard to get her attention. That's not why I feel the need to hover. I sense her slipping away, and the notion makes me want to rip the cheap wood paneling off the walls of this joint.

I don't deserve her, but the thought of losing her makes me crazy.

"Here you go." Sal returns and hands Nessa what looks like a screwdriver. He passes me another pint of beer. "The guys and I were just talking about the lack of food variety around here. What do you think, Ness? Any good Filipino restaurants nearby?"

He's trying to lighten the mood, and I don't blame him. The tension is so thick it's choking.

Nessa looks distracted for a moment, then says, "Sure, there are a couple of places." She rattles off the names of restaurants in town I'm familiar with, but have never been to.

Should I have paid more attention? Nessa's a mix, like me. But instead of being part Washoe like me and my friends, Nessa's dad is Filipino, her mother British. I never asked her how her parents met, or why they settled in San Francisco. Never wanted to get that personal. It would have been too easy to cross the line with her from friendship into something more.

I've wanted Nessa from the first moment I met her, but she's a good girl. And I'm no boy next door.

"So did your parents hook you up with the good stuff growing up?" Sal asks.

Nessa's heritage isn't that easy to figure out. Her skin is light with olive tones, her hair black, but her face is heart-shaped, almost elfin, and not easy to define as one nationality over another. If Sal knows she's part Filipino, he must know her well. And that bothers me. Maybe I *should* worry about this guy.

Nessa gives him a small smile and shakes her head. "I ate at Filipino restaurants like everyone else. My mom did the cooking. If she was going native, I got bangers and mash and toad-in-the-hole at home. Marmite was a mainstay in our fridge."

Sal scrunches his face when Nessa explains what Marmite is. The only reason I'm familiar with the condiment is because I've been to Nessa's place more times than I can count. Of course I've scoured her fridge for food. There's a reason I always cook. I have a fast metabolism. I'm pretty much hungry all the time, and Nessa's fridge doesn't escape my pillaging.

We play a few more rounds of Cornhole, and the tension between me and Nessa eases. She high-fives Sal after sliding her last sandbag home and walks toward me, not smiling, but not scowling either. She stops to take a sip of her drink.

"Ready to leave?"

Her lower lip slides into her mouth, as if she's biting it from the inside. "You go ahead. Don't let me keep you if there's someplace you need to be."

I don't like the implication in her tone, or the fact that she thinks I'll leave here without her. "I should get you home."

She spears me with a look. "I'm fine. I can take care of myself."

"Course you can. I just figured you were ready to go." *Hoped* is more like it.

Indecision plays on her face, and she looks over at her friends. They've divided up the sandbags and are preparing for another game.

"I guess I am tired. It's been a long day."

"Sure." I grab her sweatshirt. Her brow furrows—there's a chance I'm pushing her out the door—but she reaches for her purse and walks over to the guys.

Sal gives her a hug, and I grind my teeth. He seems like a decent guy. I'm just not used to random dudes touching Nessa. I don't want her hurt by *anyone*—including me. And if I'm being honest, the idea of another guy touching her makes me want to crush something.

We head back silently to Blue Casino, past the sliding glass front doors, and around the side of the building to the parking garage where the employees park. I steer Nessa to my gray four-by-four, and she stops suddenly.

"My car's a few rows over. We should part here. Thanks for walking me back. I'll see you tomorrow?"

"Whoa." I shake my head. "You're not driving home."

"What are you talking about?"

"Nessa, you weigh about a buck, and I just watched you down three drinks. I'm driving. I'll take you to your car in the morning."

"You've had as much to drink as I have."

"And I weigh almost twice what you do. After two hours at Farley's, I'm sober as a judge."

She glances away as if considering. She can't argue that logic. "Fine, but I'll get my roommate to give me a ride in the morning. You don't need to pick me up."

Whatever. As long as she comes home with me... to her place... to be dropped off...Really, I need to find a way to block thoughts of me and Nessa hooking up. Messes with my concentration.

Can a guy be hypnotized for something like that? The way people are hypnotized to not smoke? I'll pay whatever price they ask if someone can make me less physically attracted to this girl.

I could stay away from Nessa, but that's not an option. That's a form of torture I'm not strong enough to withstand. I prefer mental agony to total deprivation.

I open the passenger door of my truck and she climbs in. I enter the driver's side and try not to notice how good she looks in my truck. Like she belongs. "So what's your roommate up to tonight?"

Nessa settles her purse at her feet and buckles herself in. "She's probably out with her new boyfriend. I haven't seen her much. She stays at his place most nights."

"So you're alone tonight?" This train of thought isn't helping. Now I'm thinking about being alone with Nessa at her place.

"I guess. Why, does it matter?"

"Doesn't matter. Just wondering."

I feel her gaze on me as I pull out of the parking lot and head onto the main road. "So who is she?" she asks.

Not this again. "Who?"

"That woman you're always meeting with."

I grip the steering wheel. "I told you. No one important."

"She looks important to you."

I glance over. Nessa is leaning against the door, her body angled as far away from me as possible, but her expression is intent.

"She's not. She's no one."

"I don't believe that, Zach. You see her at least every month. And those are just the times I've witnessed you together. Is she your girlfriend?"

"Absolutely not."

"Then who is she? Some kind of regular hookup?"

I don't answer. Because that's probably a decent description. But also inadequate. What Alexis and I have is far more warped than a hookup.

"Is that all women are to you?" She stares out the window. "I thought you were different." Her voice comes out warbly.

The sense I'm losing her returns. "There's nothing between her and me, Nessa. Not anymore."

Not after tonight, anyway.

She turns to me. "What does that mean?"

"I used to see her, but now I'm not. Can we change the subject?" I reach over and flick on the radio. A commercial blares through the speakers, and I punch the buttons to change the station.

"Why?"

I fumble with the radio, trying to find something to distract. "Why what?"

"Why do you do it?"

Frustrated, I flick off the radio and turn at the green light onto Nessa's street. "Can you be more specific?" I'm deflecting, avoiding. I really want nothing to do with this conversation. Maybe I should have called Nessa a cab. The two of us alone together does neither of us any good.

"Put up walls. Do you do it to her too?"

I pierce Nessa with a glare. "There is nothing remotely similar to what I had with her and what we have."

Nessa's eyes widen. "Right, because we're only friends."

We are more. Or we could be if I'm not careful—if I'm not strong enough. Which I *have* to be.

I've sensed Nessa's desire to be closer. I feel it too, but I don't understand why she can't see it. The things I've done, who I am—I'm no good for her.

"We're friends, Nessa. Good friends. Which is more than I have with any woman."

"You're friends with Mira," she says flatly.

Mira's a fellow Washoe I've known half my life, and yeah, we're close. But it's not the same. "Mira's like a sister. You're... different."

"Different. As in not good enough to be more. Not good enough to be family. Just not good enough. I get it, Zach."

"That's not what I meant." I pull up to Nessa's apartment, and before I can shut off the ignition, she jumps out of the cab.

"Thanks for the ride." She slams the door and runs—literally runs—across the parking lot to her apartment on the first floor. The building is a two-story with eight units. It's small, but close to the strip and work. I wait until she enters before I drop my head back against the headrest.

Nessa threw up barriers between us tonight for the first time since I've known her. She's a cheery person, and seeing her upset leaves a dull pain in my chest. She's gotta know there can never be anything between us, not after she realized what's been going on with me and Alexis. I feel like I'm losing her.

Though I never had her to begin with.

And that's the way it's supposed to be.

Chapter Three

Nessa

The last thing I want is to go to Zach's place tonight, but everyone's expecting me there for taco dinner. I tried to back out over the phone with Mira, but she whined about the cookies she'd made and how I had to taste her cooking. I caved. It hasn't been easy for Mira to let people in, and she's come so far. I couldn't say no and let her down.

I still can't believe Zach invited himself to drinks with me and Sal last night. Knowing he'd just left Blondie's hotel room all freshly showered wasn't enough? Now he's sticking his nose in my limited social life? I needed that drink with Sal—needed to take my mind off of Zach, not be reminded of how frustrated he makes me.

I can't handle it anymore. I'm not sure we can remain friends. It's killing me.

I eye the giant bottle of Cuervo I bought with last night's tip money, and stroke it like a baby. It's going to save me tonight. I slip on strappy-heeled sandals below my cuffed skinny jeans. I never leave the house without heels.

Even my trainers have a platform. Some might call me vertically challenged. At five feet, I'm compact and kickass. At least that's what I tell myself.

I tuck my loose V-neck T-shirt into the front of my jeans and slide on a leather jacket. My fingers graze a slice of Juicy Fruit in the side pocket, and I peel off the wrapper and jam it in my mouth. I pick up Cuervo baby and scan the room for anything I've forgotten before shouldering on my purse and heading out the door.

A few minutes later, I pull up to Zach's place. Only it's just Zach's truck in the driveway.

What the heck? I intentionally arrived late to avoid this situation. I don't want to be the first one here.

I take a deep breath and reach for Cuervo, which I belted into the front seat just to keep it safe. I don't care that I'm getting too old for liquid courage. I need it tonight. Things can't keep going on the way they have been. It's breaking me. Getting through this night without crying is step one.

Maybe I should leave town. Why *am* I still here? Tahoe was supposed to be a fun summer after college before I buckled down and got a real job, yet here I am in my second year. It's not because of *him*. Well, maybe a little. But I also love Lake Tahoe. It's my home, though I need to find a way to have a life outside of Zach and his friends. I tried last night, except Zach chose that moment to pay attention to me in a way he never has before.

Men. They are such an enigma.

Or maybe it's just Zach. He makes no sense. One minute he's looking at me like he could melt my clothes off with his eyes, the next he's walking out the door with a different girl.

Fine, liquid courage it is. Which means I'll need to call

an Uber to get home. Much as I hate to admit it, Zach was right. I shouldn't have considered driving after a few drinks last night. Being vertically challenged means the alcohol hits me harder. But if Zach hadn't upset me, I would have realized I'd had too much to drink. So really, it's all his fault.

There, I feel better now.

Grabbing my hobo purse, I cradle Cuervo in my arms and make my way up the stone path to Zach's small cabin. The metal roof is sloped toward the street with an entrance gable that extends all the way to the ground—very Tahoe. His place is cute, but it could use a lady's touch. The inside is boy décor, meaning everything shoved up against the walls, pictures hanging too high. Still, I admire him. As far as I know, Zach owns his place, which is pretty cool for a guy in his early twenties. He's a hard worker, and smart about investing his money...

And I need to stop thinking about how great he is because that's not helping.

Sucking in a courage-building gulp of evening air, I knock on the worn wooden surface and plaster a fake smile on my face.

Which immediately falls.

Because the door creaks open and Zach is standing there, shirtless, beads of water on his broad, muscular shoulders, his flat stomach plated with muscles.

Aw, shit.

"Pip—I mean—what's up, Ness? Come on in." He drags a towel over his short, dark hair and drapes it on his shoulder. His lips twist in a grin. "Nice bottle you got there."

I move inside, my body overly alert. I set Cuervo on the counter. "I thought we could use more," I say distractedly. "You just get out of the shower?" *Obviously.*

I'm flustered. I've seen Zach in his swim trunks a

million times, but the wet, just-showered look turns my brain to silly-girl mush.

"Yeah, sorry. Let me grab a shirt." He strides down the hall, a guy gait to his steps, and I pant, gasping in oxygen to get my brain to work again. This is so messed up.

"Where is everyone?" I call.

"Oh, yeah, about that," he says as he rounds the corner in a worn T-shirt that hugs his broad shoulders and biceps. "They're not coming."

He's barefoot, and his feet... Is there nothing on his body that isn't masculine and beautiful? Wait—

"What do you mean, they're not coming?"

We meet every Wednesday night. It's almost a ritual. I'm pretty sure they've never canceled before. Come snow or hangover, this night is a constant between Zach and his friends. And until recently, it was only Zach, Lewis, and Mira. Somehow I got included. Then Lewis's new girlfriend came along. Now taco dinner has been extended to include girlfriends, boyfriends, and friends of friends. It's a right party these days.

Zach squats and slides out a pan from below the stove, the jeans that sit low on his narrow hips hugging his muscled ass.

I look to the ceiling, praying for divine intervention. He cannot be serious about it being just the two of us. I will not survive.

He stands and reaches around me to the counter I'm leaning against. The scent of clean boy zaps my senses, his full lips inches away—this is just cruel.

I duck past him and move across the kitchen, placing a hand on Cuervo.

"Well." He mixes the chicken simmering in sauces and raps the utensil against the edge of the pot. "Gen's not feeling well, so Lewis is staying home to be with her. And Mira got called in to work."

That makes sense. Mira is on the fast track at Blue Casino. She's an assistant to one of the managers, and kicking ass and taking names. But being an important person has its drawbacks. She sometimes has to go in—often without warning—when staffing issues arise, or the crowds are bigger than anticipated for Blue gigs.

"What about Tyler?" Mira's boyfriend teaches at a community college. No reason for him to bail.

Zach scratches the back of his head and rests his hands low on his hips. "Yeahhh—nope. Tyler's out too. Has some last-minute revisions to make for his publisher."

Crap. I forgot about that. In addition to working at the community college, Tyler is also going to be a published author soon. He wrote a popular-science book that people in his field are all excited about.

Am I the only one who hasn't done much with her life? I mean, I'm happy. That's important, right? Well, mostly happy.

Not so happy right now. Alone. With Zach.

"What about Cali and Jaeger?" Is that desperation in my voice?

"Cali's got the same bug Gen has. Jaeger's playing nursemaid. I told Jaeger and Lewis they were being pussy-whipped jackasses, but they wouldn't listen." He leans against the counter, his gaze intent. "Just you and me, Ness. Think you can handle it?"

There's humor in his voice, conflicting oddly with the wariness in his gaze, as if he too isn't so happy about the circumstances.

"You could have canceled, you know."

Zach turns toward the stove. "I've been cooking for two

hours. Wasn't going to let the food go to waste. Besides, we don't need our friends to hang, do we?" He looks over his shoulder, a sweet smile on his face.

"Of course not." *So going to need that margarita.* "It will be good to spend time together." *Where's the damn blender?*

I dated good-looking guys in college, but for some reason, Zach is different. He's my friend, an affable guy, always ready to hang out, and so, so hot. I don't know what it is, but it's there, magnetic attraction—at least on my end.

I open the fridge for the margarita mix I know is there, because I make certain it's stocked for these nights, and cross to the blender, pouring it inside. "Ready for a drink?"

"Sure. Only, since it's just the two of us," he says as he reaches above the stove to a small cabinet, "let's use the good stuff." He grins, a hint of naughtiness behind it.

Lord save me from that grin. "Tapatio Blanco One-ten? What's that?"

"Birthday gift from my dad." He unscrews the top and pours a generous amount into the blender. He stops, eyeballs the liquid, and splashes out another shot.

"Your dad always give you top shelf for your birthday?" I've never heard of the stuff he's holding in his hand, but the bottle looks fancy.

"My dad taught me how to play poker for stakes when I was five." He returns the tequila to the cupboard. "He's not your typical dad. You know what he does for a living, right?"

"Not really. I've seen him visit the casino, but you've never introduced us."

Zach snorts. "Yeah, well, trust me, it's best I keep you off his radar."

I grab the ice pan from the mustard-yellow refrigerator

that predates me and hums like a steam engine, and pour ice into the blender. "He can't be that bad."

Zach crosses his arms. "No, not that bad, but he's a huge flirt. And pretty young women are his favorite prey. He's also a whale."

I shake my head with a smile. I work in a casino, wearing next to nothing. I'm used to attention from older men, younger men—sometimes women—it's a part of the job. And I have no problem calling security if someone gets handsy.

I pulse the blender until the mix is the perfect consistency of slush for my Zach-addled nerves. "What's a whale?"

"How can you work at Blue and not know what a whale is?" He stirs the rice. "A whale is a high-stakes gambler. Which isn't what you might think. My dad's got cash now, but he's gained and lost fortunes. It's only been recently that he's come into his stride. We struggled growing up— cash happy to cash poor in a blink. I hated that lifestyle. It's the reason I never gamble."

I hand him a glass of margarita. "But you're a dealer. How do you stand it?"

"I don't *love* it, but it's a job and it pays well. I took business courses at the community college for a while and wasn't into it. Blue pays the bills. I've been able to save and buy this place, and I plan to buy another."

"Another house? Why?"

"Investment income. One to live in, one to rent." He takes a swig of his drink and quirks his brow. "Good stuff."

I glance at the glass in my hand and take a gulp as well. "Smooth. Your dad knows his tequila."

He rolls his eyes. "Too well." Zach pulls down plates and nods toward the table. "Ready to eat?"

The conversation flows during dinner. I'm relaxed and not nervous the way I was when I first arrived. The easiness I have with Zach is partly why we've remained friends for so long, despite my unrequited lust for him. I'm bummed that he has no interest in anything more than friendship, but I'd hate to lose what we have. It's a frustrating, no-win situation.

We talk for most of the meal about Zach's dad, who seems like a pretty fascinating character. "Do they really set him up in fancy suites?" I set my fork on the plate to save room in my belly for another margarita, which I pour from the half-empty blender we brought to the table.

"Yup." Zach polishes off what must be his fifth or sixth taco.

"Does he have a driver and everything?"

I've seen the high rollers at our casino. They're no joke. They usually have an entire entourage wherever they go.

"Nah. He travels the country in his Mercedes."

"Oh, that's all?" I laugh, and Zach does too. Most people don't cruise around in luxury vehicles making a living off gambling.

"I'm just his deadbeat kid living in a dump of a place." He wipes his mouth with his napkin, a subtle smile on his face that doesn't reach his eyes.

"That can't be what he really thinks."

Zach piles empty dishes together. "Pretty much, but it's fine."

"Hold on—it's not fine. You're smart and kind, and you own your house. You're a hard worker..." My voice trails off as I realize what I'm doing. The things I'm saying. If Zach didn't know I liked him as more than friends, he might have a clue now.

He grins. "Cutie."

I sit back. "Don't call me that." I grab my drink and take a gulp that's too big, my head stinging from mild brain freeze.

When I look up, Zach's frowning. "What's wrong with 'cutie'?"

"It's something you'd say to a little girl."

"No. It's something I'd say to a girl who's too tempting for her own good." He stands abruptly and takes the dishes to the sink. "You finished?" He glances over, the frown he wore a second ago gone.

It takes me a minute to register his question, because I'm still stuck on the preceding sentence. I nod stiffly.

What did he mean, I'm too tempting for my own good? He's never acknowledged an attraction to me. I glance at my margarita. Am I drunk? Is this my second or third? I'm sensing a solid buzz... *Third, for sure.*

I bus the pots and pans and wrap up the leftovers.

Zach puts the last of the dishes in the dishwasher and turns it on. "Did you bring your bathing suit?"

He has a hot tub in his backyard, which is far and away the most expensive item in his house. The hot tub is new, unlike the used furniture scattered about.

I shake my head, and he scratches the faint five o'clock shadow on the side of his jaw. "Okay—well, I've got something you can wear."

"It's all right. I should get going anyway."

"Why?" he says. "You got a hot date?" His words are a jest, but there's no modulation to his tone, and I get the feeling he wouldn't be happy if I did. Which is strange.

When I ran from his truck yesterday, I was convinced there could never be anything between us. Why all of a sudden would he care if I dated somebody else?

"No, but I should call a cab. It's getting late. I didn't mean to, but I think I drank too much again."

Okay, maybe I intended to numb myself with alcohol, but then I got more comfortable the more we talked. I'm not sure how I overdrank without realizing it. I'm not smashed, but I'm not sober enough to drive.

"A-hundred-and-ten-proof tequila will do that to you. Sorry, I should have said something. We'll down some water and sweat it off in the hot tub. I'd give you a ride, but I'm feeling it myself. If we wait a bit, I can take you home. Come on." He walks out of the kitchen. "I'll find you something to wear."

I hear the logic in his words, but I'm not sure about the hot tub. Removing clothes, just the two of us? Not such a good idea. Not with the desperate way I've been feeling these last couple of days, and the things he's saying tonight. Which have gone to my head and filled it with stupid hope.

Even so, I follow Zach to his bedroom. He rustles around in one of the dresser drawers and pulls out a high school rugby shirt. "This'll do. You can use the master bath to change."

I walk into the bathroom and take off my clothes. I actually wore a pretty bra and panty set tonight. It's emerald green and satin, and stands out against my light olive complexion. And it's way too sexy for getting in a hot tub with Zach. Good thing the dark shirt will hide what I'm wearing beneath.

After pulling on the shirt that smells like him—dammit—I set my clothes on the toilet seat and pad back out. Zach's in board shorts I've seen him wear at the beach. For a moment, his gaze skims my bared legs.

"Let's go," he says, and tosses me a towel, the spark in his eyes gone.

Good, because if he starts looking at me like that, we're in trouble.

He heads down the hallway toward the living room and the back door that leads to the hot tub. We've all talked about hot-tubbing at Zach's a million times, and I'm pretty sure the guys have stayed late after taco dinner to do just that, but for some reason, I never have.

Zach doesn't bother turning on the porch light. Once we get into the hot tub, he pushes a couple of buttons and a light at the bottom of the tub turns on, along with bubbles. I sink into one of the bucket seats, and he hands me a bottled water. My shoulders and the rest of my body relax, sending a shiver through me.

"This was a good idea. Forget I suggested going home," I say.

He chuckles. "This baby was my one splurge when I bought the place."

He's not kidding. The furniture in his house has to be second- or third-hand. "I'm kind of fond of your couch. The blue velvet is rather cozy."

A wide grin spreads across his face. "Isn't it? My grandma handed that one down. Been in the family forever."

I shake my head. "She had good taste—fifty years ago."

His grin remains and his eyes twinkle in the dim light. "You know, Ness, I'm not gonna be offended if you want to take that clingy shirt off and relax in your bra and panties. I promise not to jump you. It's not like I haven't seen you in a bikini before."

True. My bikini has about as much fabric as my panty set. "You could pretend you think I'm pretty. Girls like to feel beautiful sometimes, even from their guy friends."

"First off, you know you're beautiful. Second, that would be crossing the line."

I let out a deep sigh. I heard the *beautiful,* which made me really happy—for about one second. Until he said he'd never cross the line.

"Just for argument's sake, what's wrong with crossing the line?" *Am I really going there?* I'll probably regret it in the morning, but for now... "Friends date all the time."

Zach shifts in his seat and pops the top off his water. "I like our friendship. I wouldn't want to ruin it."

"Because you never stay with anyone for more than one night?"

This pattern of his has kept us apart and kept him single. It's a double-edged sword. On the one hand, if he's single, he's available. On the other hand, he never commits, so it's a moot point. I don't want a one-nighter with Zach. I want more.

He scowls.

"What? It's true. Name the last person you dated more than once—"

"That would be—"

"Who you hadn't already slept with."

His mouth clamps shut. So nailed him on that one.

He scrubs the side of his jaw, his telltale nervous tic. "Fine, so I don't do the romantic thing."

"Is that what you call it?"

His thick, broad shoulder lifts in a shrug. "I'm just not much of a relationship guy."

"You have long-term friendships," I point out.

"That's different."

I don't know why I'm pushing it. Must be that 110-proof tequila, but I can't seem to make my mouth stop. "I bet we could keep a relationship going." My heart thunders in my chest at the admission.

He stares at me as if analyzing a curious puzzle. "Where are you going with this, Nessa?"

I shrug like he did. "Just that we're friends, and if we wanted to be more, I bet it would work out."

He's silent for a long moment, then, "Well, we'll never know."

My face heats. I know there's something between us—have felt it all along. But for some reason, this time I can't back down. "In that case, since you feel so platonic about me, it shouldn't matter what I'm wearing."

I grab the hem of my shirt in frustration and pull the fabric over my head. It lands with a loud *splat* on the wooden porch.

Zach sits forward, his eyes going wide. "Wait, what?"

"Ahhh, much better. You said so yourself. I have no reason to worry about you jumping me."

He squirms, his eyes dropping below my chin for a split second, only to flash back to my face.

He rests against the side of the tub and his mouth turns up in a grin. "Of course. I already said you should lose the shirt."

God, he's infuriating. He's actually going to act like he isn't attracted to me, when my gut and his squirming tell me he is?

I'm tired of wanting a guy who holds me at arm's length. I may be off my rocker, but two can play this game. I reach behind and unclasp my bra.

This time, Zach splashes water in his effort to sit forward. "What are you doing?"

I ignore him and drag the straps down my arms. My silk

and lace panties go next, landing with a light *plop* on top of the shirt I discarded.

My hands are shaking. This is an extreme measure to prove a point. It's not normal for me to strip to get a guy's attention. In fact, I've never done anything like it before. If Zach wasn't such a stubborn mule, I wouldn't have to.

Taking a deep breath, I close my eyes, sinking deeper in the water, but the tips of my nipples buoy up for a second, breaching the surface. My eyes pop open. "Oops."

Zach is frozen, his gaze on my body. "Nessa." His voice is a strangled growl.

"This shouldn't be a big deal. You said you're not attracted to me," I remind him.

"I didn't say that."

"You said there's nothing to worry about, and that I should make myself comfortable."

"I didn't think you were gonna *skinny-dip*. Christ." He scrubs a wet hand down his face.

"You told me you weren't interested." My tone is challenging now.

"Those weren't my words."

"It was implied."

Zach fingers his hair forcefully, making it stick up in spiky, damp clumps. "I think you should put the shirt back on."

"Why? You'll still be able to see my nip—"

"*Don't* say it."

"—ples. What's wrong, Zach? Got a problem?"

I don't know why I'm enjoying his discomfort, but I really, really am.

I prop my foot on the edge of the hot tub and cross my legs at the ankle. Zach's gaze darts to my feet and roams up, then closes off abruptly when he shuts his eyes tight. "I'm a weak man, Nessa. Don't do this."

"You don't seem like a weak man, Zach. We've been friends for over a year, and you've never once made a move."

"Well, not for a lack of wanting!"

My heart pounds in my chest, and for a second, I can't catch my breath. He's never admitted to feeling an attraction.

I throw up my hands. "I don't understand. What are you waiting for?"

"Nessa," he pleads. "You've got to stop."

The look on his face—he's serious. He doesn't want me. Like, *really* doesn't want me. Not if he's begging me to put my clothes back on. He may find me attractive, because I'm a naked girl in his hot tub, but he's *not interested.*

My mouth goes dry and I choke on the pain that's risen from my chest. I stand abruptly to escape, remember I'm fully naked, and drop back down. I cover my face with my hands and push back the tears rushing to my eyes.

Why did I do this? I'm the stubborn one. I took it too far, and now look what's happened. I've made a complete ass of myself.

"You're killing me," he says in a weary voice.

Water swishes around me, and then I'm being lifted up and onto his lap, his arms encircling me. My first thought, removed from the despair, is electric sensation everywhere. My naked skin on top of his muscular, warm lap, his large chest pressed against the side of my breast. But I tamp it down, because attraction and intimacy aren't what he wants. He's comforting me, trying to be a good guy. I'm the one throwing myself at him and having dirty thoughts while sitting on his lap. *God, will I never learn?*

His strong fingers tuck a lock of hair behind my ear. He

leans me against his body and pets my head. Like I'm a little girl.

My previous anger sparks at those brotherly touches—so tired of it. Until he lifts me up and palms the bottom of my ass, fitting me more squarely on his lap. *There.*

He's thick and long, and the electric throbbing I've been trying to ignore increases. I peel my hands from my face and dare to look at him.

His gaze isn't brotherly. It's focused, his jaw taut, but when he leans forward and kisses my cheek, his lips are soft and gentle.

My heart pounds so hard I go lightheaded. "What are you doing?"

Zach inhales deeply, his body pressing closer to mine—igniting, inflaming. "Making a move."

His head descends, his mouth capturing mine, and this time, I wrap my arms around his shoulders and kiss him back. Hard and deep, unleashing everything I feel for him.

I cling to him, touching his neck, his face, everywhere I can, because I've wanted him for so long. The kiss is hot—lips and tongue, sending flutters throughout my body. My previous worries disappear. Nothing else matters but the two of us together.

A low groan erupts from him. His hand roams up and down my waist, grazing the breast now plastered to his chest.

Yes. More.

I break our kiss for only a second and lift up to straddle his waist.

Zach grips the small of my back and drags me closer, his length pressing against the most sensitive part of me. "Nessa, we shouldn't do this."

It takes me a minute to register his words. What's he

talking about? He can't kiss me like that and say he doesn't want it. But he just told me that he only wanted to be friends.

My confusion must show on my face, because he says, "But I don't care if it's right or not. Tired of fighting it." His mouth slams against mine, then gentles, his hands cradling my face. And I stop thinking altogether. I'm tired of worrying about whether this attraction is only in my head. I feel *this*. His hands and mouth on my body. That's my reality, and I'm tuning everything else out.

Zach stands and climbs out of the hot tub with me in his arms, my legs wrapped around his waist. He's holding me against him, one thick arm tucked beneath my ass, his mouth never stopping its seduction of my lips.

We reach the sliding glass door and he stops. I feel him dip, then shift from side to side.

It's cold out, but his body is warm. Hot. His heart is pounding against my breasts. He drags the slider open, then takes less than a nanosecond to close it behind us. And that's when I see his bathing suit on the ground. *That's what he was doing.*

Doing...? *Are* we doing this? I want to, but does he? I'm overthinking it again.

I press my hands to either side of the face I adore with every ounce of my being—his square jaw, the chin with the slightest indentation, the one ear that sticks out a touch farther than the other—the hungry look in his eyes. With him holding me as he makes his way down the hallway, we're almost nose to nose. "We don't have to do this, Zach. We can stay friends."

"Too late for that."

The next thing I know, I'm flying through the air.

My legs flail, and a squeak erupts from my mouth a split second before I land with a bounce on his bed.

Zach comes down on top of me, supporting his weight with his arms while he eases into the cradle of my thighs. "You okay?"

I didn't land hard—that's not what he's referring to. He's asking permission. Because he's not a jerk. He cares, even if he denied it until now.

"Yeah." I reach up and run my fingers across his collarbone, over the sloped ridges of his cut upper arms. Zach has the best shoulders. I could stare at them all day, if I didn't enjoy his pretty, pretty face so much.

Which reminds me—I run the pad of my finger over his lower lip, and he nips it with his teeth, then scoots down. He kisses the center of my chest, his lips sliding to my nipple, where he pushes the side of my breast up with one hand and wraps his mouth around the tip.

I squirm, shifting against his waist, seeking more friction. Zach takes his time, wreaking havoc with his tongue and not giving a damn that he's driving me insane—the way he's done for the last year and a half. Though I will happily put up with this form of insanity and live a contented lady, I wouldn't mind moving things along.

If I could just get him to shift a little north so that he lines up with my—

He reaches down and grabs my ass. "I've wanted to do that since the day I met you." He kneads the curve, then slides his palm up and down as if mapping it out. "I own this ass."

Interesting. I never took him for the possessive sort. "Oh yeah? Well, I claim these shoulders. And your muscled butt, and that thick, long—"

My words get cut off by a kiss so tender it stuns me. And I don't want to talk anymore. I want to be held by the guy who baffles me one minute and makes me half crazed the next.

Zach's hands roam, deliberate and focused on every inch of my body. It's been a while since I've been with a guy, but I don't remember it feeling like this. Everywhere his hands touch has my body shaking, craving more.

He reaches over the edge of the bed in the midnight-darkened room and tears a condom open. Leaning to the side, he slides it on. My heart races at the glimpse of his flat stomach, muscular leg, and that part of him reaching for me, wanting me. He settles back, but he's still not where I need him.

"Are you sure you don't want to scooch up a little?"

"I'm good." He kisses my chin, the curve of my cheek, the edge of my lips, finally settling on my mouth, where he loves me with such intensity that I wonder if I've been wrong all along. That Zach has always felt more, and has been holding back.

I run my hands down the contours of his wide chest and stomach, reaching around to his ass, where I grab him and yank him up. He's way bigger than me and it's not like I actually budge him, but he finally scoots until I feel the head of him where my body is throbbing.

"I'm not going to hurt you, Nessa." It's an oath. As if he's convincing himself. And then he slides into me and all I can think is, *He's mine. For now.* And hopefully longer, if I can prove this thing between us is right.

The love I have for Zach cloaks us. There's no way he can't sense it. And I'm too far gone to pretend otherwise.

I want to tell him how I feel—so much love—but I say nothing. And then I stop thinking about anything except for his fingers lightly squeezing my nipples, his hand curved around my ass just like he said—as if he owns it—using that part of me to guide himself in and out at just the right angle.

My breath hitches when he hits a certain spot. And being the suddenly perceptive guy that he is tonight, he stays there, working it over and over.

Stars flicker across my vision. My body convulses as the longest orgasm in the history of orgasms suddenly overwhelms me.

"Oh God," I say as I start to come down from a high I've never experienced before.

"Nope, just me. And by the way, we're not finished."

Zach pumps in and out in an easy pattern until my breathing changes from the gasping, panting mess it was to something resembling normal.

"Can't hold it any longer," he murmurs, and angles slightly, finding some new position that must feel good because he's already coming, groaning and shaking above me, his mouth on my neck, sucking in counterpoint to the pleasure down below.

His breaths slowly calm, and he sprinkles kisses on my neck and face, as if he can't get enough. He eases to the side, tucking me up close to him.

We lie like that for a few minutes, and I must fall asleep. The next thing I know, he's getting out of bed and walking to the bathroom. I'm so sleepy and sated I can't move, so I don't. I lie there like a lump.

The mattress dips after what feels like seconds, and Zach wraps me in a body hug. I nod off, wondering if it's all a dream.

And if I'll wake up to the dream, or to reality.

Chapter Four

I'm utterly relaxed, except that my mouth feels like I slept with cotton in it all night. I blink a few times and look around the room. My eyes widen.

I'm at Zach's. And last night... *Shit!*

I glance over without moving my face, afraid I'll wake him. And then I do look, because he's passed out on his stomach, pressed up against me, one arm bent under his head. I want to reach out and touch him, he's so cute. There's a throw blanket he must have tossed over us at some point, because we never even made it up to the pillows. We're lying in the middle of the bed, his feet dangling off the end.

I'd like to blame it on the tequila, but I didn't have *that* much to drink last night. The only thing I can use to defend myself for winding up in his bed is that I was a starved girl. Once I had access to the guy I've been dreaming about, I gorged—and promptly fell asleep.

Geez, I'm like a man. Take what I want and pass out.

My stomach sinks. What if he regrets it? I mean, I got naked in front of him. And then cried. Holy crap, what if what we shared was *guilt* sex out of some kind of pity he felt toward me?

I should leave. Get out of here before he wakes. Because if he wakes and looks uncomfortable, or tries to shoo me to the door, it would break my heart. I can't deal with that right now. I need a shower. And a toothbrush. And some sugar at hand before I tackle that kind of letdown.

Light streams through the window, but it's faded and blue, as if it's still early out. I slide my hand across the mattress to the side of the bed, and glance over to see if he stirs.

No signs of life. I slowly ease myself out of bed and stand, watching him like he's a rabid animal about to pounce. I'm so intent on searching for possible movement, I'm not looking where I'm going.

My pinkie toe strikes the foot of the bedframe. Pain bursts up my leg and it's all I can do to keep quiet.

Son of a bitch!

Hopping, I hold my toe, lose my balance, and land on my ass. I crawl toward the bathroom and spy over my shoulder to make sure Zach's still asleep.

I am an idiot, on the ground, stealing away like a thief in the night.

And I'm totally okay with that right now.

I quietly close the bathroom door until only a crack stands between me and the other room. Holding on to the counter, I pull myself up and catch my breath. I prop my foot on the toilet seat cover and check out my pinky toe. It's bright red and swelling. Awesome.

Dressing quickly—without my bra and panties, dammit, because they're still in a damp pile by the hot tub —I glance in the mirror, and holy hell. I have mascara smudged below my eyes and—I press my finger to the side of my neck—a red splotch on my skin. Is that a hickey? He *marked* me?

Wow. My face warms, my belly clenching. Last night was—I fan myself with a hand. I really need to get out of here before I do something stupid like crawl back into bed with him. He could very well regret last night.

I quickly remove as much of the mascara below my eyes as I can and stare at my hair. It's knotted and sticking up, as though I've rubbed it on the side of a balloon. I don't remember rubbing my head into the mattress, but well, I was preoccupied. Good Lord, I've never felt that good before. My body still hums from what Zach did to me. No wonder the ladies like him.

Gack! I hate thinking of him with other women. What if he goes right back to doing what he's always done, hooking up and calling me Pipsqueak? How will I deal with it? I brace my hands on the counter and take a deep breath. This is exactly why I'm leaving before I'm forced to face truths too difficult to contemplate in my lovesick state.

I hobble out of the bathroom, my shoes and purse in hand. There's no way I can walk in heels with my toe twice its normal size. Plus, I'm in stealth mode. I don't need noisy heels waking Zach.

He's in the same exact position he was when I left the bed. He hasn't moved, his muscled leg peeking out from under the blanket. My chest tightens.

I hate leaving him, but I can't suppress the fear he might regret last night, or worse, treat me like any other woman he's slept with. I couldn't handle that.

What if our night together ruined everything?

* * *

Zach

I blink away sleep.

Something isn't right. Staring at the closet door, I try to figure out what feels off...

I sit up abruptly and glance at the empty spot beside me. "Nessa?" I call.

No answer. I leap out of bed and pull on gym shorts. I stride across the bedroom and nudge the bathroom door open the rest of the way. She's not there, and neither are the clothes she folded and placed with her purse.

I walk down the hallway, my heart racing. My limbs are like liquid, serene and calm, while my chest is tight and anxious. I've never felt so conflicted after a night with a woman. But then, this isn't just any woman. It's *Nessa*. And she's not where I left her.

She's not in the kitchen or the living room, and the chain isn't on the front door. I never forget to attach the chain before I go to bed. Though I wasn't exactly thinking of burglars last night. There are a lot of things I *forgot* last night. Like my promise to never go there with Nessa.

But I went there anyway.

And it was amazing.

I knew I'd been cheapening myself with Alexis and the women I slept with afterward to cleanse myself of the guilt, but nothing prepared me for making love to Nessa. She would never use me, and I held nothing back. Because with this girl, I am myself.

Since the day I lost my virginity to Alexis, sex with women has never been serious. With Nessa, there was none of that crap. I care so much about her, and now that we've crossed the line, I'm not letting go.

I'm also about to go out of my mind if I don't figure out where she went. Not a fan of her running out on me.

I scan the living room and storm toward the sliding glass door, peering out. The hot tub is uncovered. The bubbles shut down after a certain amount of time, but the light is still on. I didn't even shut the sliding glass door all the way when I carried Nessa inside. That's how much of a rush I was in to get her to my bed.

I open the slider and walk out in my shorts, the crisp morning air and cool deck chilling my feet and skin. I shut everything down and spy Nessa's panties and bra by the hot tub.

I smile and walk over to pick them up. They're sexy as hell, and I would have liked to see her in them, but not as much as I enjoyed seeing her out of them. I wring them out and set them along with my swim trunks across a chair to dry, and go back inside. Nessa didn't even stop to grab her underwear before she left. Was she upset?

We were plastered against each other all night. I know, because I woke a few times and watched her sleep, until exhaustion stole my ability to creeper-stare at the beautiful girl next to me.

How could she leave without saying goodbye? If she thinks we're going back to only being friends, she's mistaken. And I'm going to show her how wrong she is. Just as soon as I find her. Think I'll enjoy proving how well we fit together.

I don't know why I fought things between us for so long, but I'm finished with all that. I may not have planned this, but I'll do whatever it takes to make her happy. Nessa deserves everything.

I check the time. *Eight.* She couldn't have been gone long, because the last time I woke it was five in the morning, and she was sound asleep. I'd rolled over and tucked her sexy little body up against mine. Took all my strength not to wake her too.

My lips twitch into a smile. I'm striding toward my bedroom, preparing to take a shower and hunt her down, when a loud knock sounds at the front door. Thinking it's her and that she's returned, I swing the door open with that ridiculous grin plastered to my face.

A whoosh of disappointment washes over me. "What's up, Dad?"

"Someone had a late night." He brushes past me and heads into the kitchen.

My father is average height, with broad shoulders and a few extra pounds, thanks to all the casino comps he gets. But he's a good-looking older dude, or so I've been told.

I hover near the door. This better not take long. Can't leave things the way they are with Nessa running off like that. Did I upset her somehow? Maybe I'll swing by Muffin Top and grab bagels and coffee on my way to her place.

"What do you have to drink around here?" my dad asks as he opens and closes cupboard doors.

"There's orange juice in the fridge and some milk."

Dad grabs the orange juice, frowning. He zeros in on the cupboard above the fridge and finds the vodka I keep there.

"Dad, I've got somewhere to be. Can we catch up later?"

He raises an eyebrow, and I sigh. When my dad digs in his heels, there's no budging him. I walk toward the kitchen and sink into the chair at the peninsula.

"What have you been up to?" He pours orange juice in a tumbler and adds a heavy splash of Absolut. He raises the glass to me and quirks his brow. I shake my head.

"Work. And work. More work."

"Can't only be work." He glances around, his gaze narrowing on my swim trunks and Nessa's panties on the chair outside. "Who's the girl that left this morning?"

Leave it to my father's powers of observation, honed by years of gambling, to scope out the incriminating items lying around. "How do you know she left this morning?"

"You've got a fire lit under your ass, and you're"—he raises his hand and gestures at the side of his face—"peaked."

"Seriously, you're going there? Dad, I don't want to talk about my personal life. We've never discussed it. No need to start now."

He hands me a glass of orange juice, sans vodka. "Well, maybe we should. You still spending time with Alexis? What's she up to?"

Fuck. I do not want to talk about Alexis. Not while I'm still high on Nessa.

Sometimes I wonder how much my dad suspects about my past with Alexis. "I don't know what she's up to. I don't keep tabs."

As far as I'm concerned, whatever Alexis and I had is over. And I plan to tell her so as soon as possible.

"Too bad—she's got a hot little body on her."

Now he's just goading me. I don't for one minute think my dad is after Alexis. She might be physically attractive, but I can't see that anymore. All I see is what she's like on the inside—something my dad saw years ago when he warned my mom about being friends with her.

"If Alexis is so great, why don't you keep in touch with her?" I snap, and grab the glass he filled for me.

"Out of my league. She likes 'em young."

I choke on my juice. *Fuck.*

Dad slams back his screwdriver. "Well, I'm outta here. Got an appointment in Reno. Go find *your girl*." He winks.

"Try not to lose your shirt. Luck doesn't last forever."

"Bite your tongue. It's lasted me six years and counting. And it ain't luck, it's *skill*."

He walks out and I drop my head into my hands.

No doubt there's skill, but my dad has had his share of bad runs that almost put us in the poorhouse when I was in high school. Back then I had a part-time job in the afternoons and on weekends. I couldn't add more hours without dropping out of school, and I wasn't about to do that. I'm no genius, but I knew I needed a diploma to get anywhere. Thank God my dad's rough-streak didn't last long. He had more faith than I did, and won some big hands at the blackjack tables while rubbing shoulders with Alexis's exhusband.

Alexis divorced her husband when I was in high school —and took a good portion of his cash when she did. Now she plays the tables as often as my dad. She's smart, though. She gambles *other* people's money and lives off her cushy alimony payments. Alexis used to tell me I was the most important person in her life. It didn't bother me that she dated other men. I thought we had something special, and I was pleased as punch to be called her favorite. That shows how young and stupid I was when our affair began.

Now, I don't care. I'm so sick of whatever it is we've been doing. Literally sick. The sneaking around, the crap she tells me to keep me strung along... I'm over it. What I want is so clear now. And this time, I'm reaching for it.

I shower off the filth that thinking about Alexis leaves on my skin, and dress quickly, my need to find Nessa and ensure everything is okay stronger than ever. But because this has been a hell of a morning, Alexis walks in the front door as I'm tucking my wallet in the back pocket of my jeans.

And it's my fault, because I stupidly gave her a key to the place years ago.

There goes what's left of my Nessa high—the beautiful feeling she infused into me last night with her gorgeous soul, taunting mouth, and incredible body. All of that lingering goodness gone the moment Alexis arrives.

"Hello, darling." She closes the door and walks up, wrapping her arms around my waist.

I ease her back, but she's got me in an arm lock. "What do you need, Alexis?"

She glances at me incredulously. "Is that any way to welcome your lover? What's gotten into you lately?" She finally steps away, probably because I'm still pushing her back.

I walk to the sofa and take a seat. Because we need to have this out. I won't put it off any longer. Everything has changed. Well, it's been changing for a while, but now I want it finalized. No way am I risking things with Nessa because of Alexis.

"Look, there were feelings in the beginning." I clasp my hands between my knees. "Or at least I think there were. I was young..."

She pouts and slides next to me, running her hand down my chest. I push it away and shift gears. Alexis is too aggressive to let down easily. "I'm not interested in a relationship with you anymore. We've both grown and changed. I should have ended things years ago. I want to end it now, and I'd appreciate my house key back."

Her expression is frozen for a split second, a hint of real fear in her eyes. Then she huffs out a breath. "You can't be serious."

"I couldn't be more serious. I wish you the best." I stand and step toward the door, hoping she'll get the hint.

I'd tell her she'll make someone happy someday, but I don't believe it after what she's put me through. Alexis is conniving, backstabbing—an all-around miserable person. I hadn't realized it until I finally came up for air. With Nessa.

The moment I kissed Nessa, my fucked-up world righted itself. *This* was how it was supposed to be. Not the cold, warped thing I'd had with Alexis, or anyone else.

"Of course we'll see each other. You don't cut ties like the ones we have." She follows me toward the door and tries to touch me again.

I grab her wrist before she makes contact, and ease it to her side. "You and I have never been together. Not like that. And no, we won't see each other again. I've moved on."

Her gaze narrows. "With who?" There's a hard edge to her tone, and I wish I hadn't said anything.

"No one for you to concern yourself with. I'm sure you want me to be happy." I don't think she gives a fuck about my happiness, but I'm trying to subtly convince her to take the high road.

"Darling, we can at least be friends, can't we?" Her words are sweet, almost warm, but I know better. She'll use any means to sink her claws into me—to make me think she cares when she really only cares for herself.

More important, *I* don't care for her anymore. "No. We can't."

She crosses her arms over her chest. "This is ridiculous. What does this little bitch have on you? Don't tell me she won't share. We both know you're not the commitment type."

I haven't been, but that doesn't mean I can't be. The hookups I've had, in between nights with Alexis, were all a means to cleanse the filth, yet they left their own inky stain. I didn't care for those girls, other than wanting to make sure they had a good time and got home safely. There's never been anyone I've wanted to commit to, until Nessa.

There's no way I'm sharing Nessa. Wouldn't even consider it.

And if Nessa will have me, I'm all in.

Chapter Five

I pull up to Nessa's apartment around ten, after shoving Alexis out the door. I told her to mind her own damn business and stay away after she probed into who I was dating. I practically had to pry the key to my house out of her hand, but I got it back. If I hadn't, I would have paid to have the locks changed.

Ironically, in the three years since I bought the place, this morning was the first time Alexis has ever used the key. And it will be the last.

I made a quick run to Muffin Top to pick up two lattes and some pastries, hoping to share a late breakfast with Nessa. Despite my unwelcome visitors, it's still early enough that I might catch her at home. Where we can talk... and define things. Because I don't like the way she ran out without saying goodbye. Left a bad feeling in my gut.

I knock on the front door of her apartment, and her roommate answers. "Hey, Teresa. Nessa around?"

"Hi. No, she's out running errands."

I let out a low sigh. This morning isn't working out the way I expected. "You know where she went?"

"I don't. Sorry. Want me to leave a message?"

I hand Teresa one of the lattes and the bag of food. "Just tell her I'm looking for her. I already left her a message on her phone."

She juggles the bag of food. "Sure, I'll tell her you came by."

This is beginning to feel like more than Nessa and I simply missing each other. Is she avoiding me?

I walk to my truck and think back to last night—and the best sex of my life. The connection we had was intense. Was it too intense? Did I come on too strong? We're good friends, and maybe she's freaking out about what happened.

I rest my forehead on the steering wheel. "Get a grip." I need to simmer down and let her volley back with a call or text.

I'm not used to caring about whether or not I see a girl. I don't know how to handle the situation. A relationship with Nessa isn't what I set out to have. I've tried to protect her—to stay away. But it didn't work. I wanted her too badly. Now that we've gone there, there's no going back, and I don't even want to.

Tonight we're both working the Bitchin' Eighties party at Blue. If we don't connect before work, I'll ask her to meet up with me afterward. One way or another, we're hashing this thing out, because her leaving me after the best sex in the history of hot sex was not cool. And if, in the back of my mind, I know the connection has way more to do with Nessa and less to do with sex, I'm keeping it there. I'm not about to overanalyze my feelings right now. I just need the girl to answer my calls.

* * *

Nessa

I've been a nervous wreck all day. After running every errand I could find to keep from thinking about Zach, I finally checked my messages. My sister called once, and Zach called twice. Teresa said he also stopped by.

Teresa already interrogated me about where I was last night, and I'm pretty sure she knows something's up. I didn't go into details, but she's aware I spent the night at Zach's place. She's asked me about my feelings for him before. I've kept mum about it, hiding them from her the way I've done with my other friends, but my roommate is definitely on to me.

The food Zach brought me was sweet, but it could also be a peace offering for the mistake he'd made. He may not have long-lasting relationships with women (or more than one date), but he's always been a decent guy. He wouldn't straight up bail—*God*, exactly the way I did.

I was a giant wuss this morning, and I still am. I don't want to lose Zach, and I figure if I avoid him, I don't need to face it. Irrational, but effective.

A little voice in the back of my mind keeps piping up that he might actually *want* to see me. That maybe he didn't like it when I left this morning. I've been squelching it because I don't want to get my hopes up. Zach is the king of casual hookups. In any case, I'll see him tonight at Blue, because for once, we're working together in the same room. No more hiding. Time to face him.

I'm freaking out as I make my way into the casino.

Deep breath. Still fifteen more minutes before my shift begins.

I take the elevator to the executive floor. I arrived a few minutes early to ask Mira a question. It's the beginning of my shift and the tail end of hers, but I should be able to catch her.

I wave to Gayle, the receptionist, as I pass through the executive lobby. Word is that Gayle used to be a cocktail waitress until she landed an admin position. She's wearing a professional pinstriped navy suit, but as always, she's got on heavy makeup, and her hair is bright red. I can totally picture Gayle downstairs at one time with the rest of the waitresses. And I'm hoping to follow in her footsteps—with an executive job, not the red hair dye.

I wind my way down two corridors to Mira's office. She has one of those cramped, no-windows spaces. I'd like to say it's homey, but really, it's not. One wall is taken up by a giant whiteboard filled with dates and events spread across it, the other houses a large, half-dead plant.

Mira glances up as I walk in, and smiles. "What's up, girl?" She shoves on the heels she tucked under her desk and gives me a hug.

I razz her for not showing up last night after she guilt-tripped me into going to taco dinner, and she gestures to her desk. It's piled high with folders.

"Is that what you were working on?"

"Yes." She sighs. "Blue has been suffering from a staffing shortage these last few months. We've got a new guy in hospitality, but the rest of the work falls on me or Hayden. How's the floor? I take it you're working tonight, since you're here."

"Yeah, I'll be in the club." No need to tell Mira I'm working the Bitchin' Eighties party. She's more up on Blue events than anyone I know.

"I actually came in a few minutes early to ask you some-thing." I tuck a lock of long hair behind my ear, suddenly nervous. "Can you let me know if a position opens at Blue that you think I'd be qualified for?" I rattle off the internships I completed in college.

It's promising that the casino needs more support, but I have little to no real job experience. Still, I'm hoping something pops up that could get me in with the executives.

I can't believe I've been working as a waitress for more than a year. My parents hounded me when I first moved to Lake Tahoe about getting a "real job" after they paid for college. A year and half later, I'm realizing that time got away from me. It's been so long, even my parents have gone silent. But I'm ready to branch out.

"I'll check out the other casinos as well. I just wanted to touch base with you first, since I'm already working at Blue. It can't hurt to have floor experience, right?"

"Absolutely not. And you're being ridiculous. Of course I'll help. Actually..." She taps her chin. "I have something in mind. Could be really good." More tapping.

She's making me nervous. "Whatever it is, I'm up for it. I'm totally flexible."

"Good, because there's just one hitch. It's not a paid position."

* * *

Tonight I'm in a killer eighties getup, complete with leg warmers and an off-the-shoulder sequined top. A short, stretchy black miniskirt completes the outfit. Thankfully, because it's a themed night, I'm getting away with wearing my platform tennis shoes. One of my errands this morning was a trip to the doctor. Turns out I didn't break my toe this morning—it only felt like it.

That'll teach me to have a pseudo one-night stand and sneak out in the wee hours of the morning.

My toe feels like crap, and if it weren't for this eighties night, I'd have to call in sick. No way could I work in heels. Platform sneakers, though, I can handle.

I attack the last of the hooks on my bustier—because even in eighties garb, Blue still has us boobed up to our chins. I suck in and spin it around so it's holding up what little God gave me. I'm not the most well-endowed girl, but even I have a rack in Blue uniforms.

The cocktail waitress outfits are pretty and fun to wear, but I'd have no problem hanging them up for stylish business attire. I'm not going to lie, when I stopped by Mira's office before my shift, I was thinking of a paid position. But the internship she told me about sounds perfect. So perfect, I could temporarily look past the unpaid aspect. I'd be working in the marketing department, assisting the manager.

Interning for a few hours before my waitressing shift begins would make me busy, but if all went well, it could lead to a solid paid position. And unlike most companies offering entry-level marketing jobs, the casino actually pays well, which is why they recruit through internships.

It's time I put myself out there again, or I might end up a forty-year-old waitress at Blue Casino with dyed black hair and corns on my feet. Waitressing is easy, the people are nice, and the money is good. And it's nothing like the exciting marketing career I envisioned when I graduated from college.

So many Lake Tahoe waitresses have made careers out of it. They're living in paradise with good pay, and it's not so bad. But it's not me. I'm not sure how it happened. How I got stuck this last year. And after making what could be the biggest mistake of all by sleeping with one of my best friends—who happens to be the guy I'm stupidly in love with—I need a change. I need to move on. My love life might be in turmoil, but I can take a stand with my career.

I walk through the casino on my way to the Blue club, and several patrons turn their heads and gawk. Hopefully that's a sign of solid tips in my future. This eighties outfit is going to pay the bills. And being busy at work is a good thing, because I'm freaking out about seeing Zach.

I walk past the bouncer in front of the velvet rope to the club. There's no one in line, but it's still early. People won't begin pouring in for another hour.

The lights are dim inside, and it's difficult to see. I grab a Juicy Fruit from my cash caddy and jam it into my mouth, chewing feverishly. As soon as it's more crowded, I'll have to spit out the gum and act professional. Until then, I'm working out my anxiety through my jaw.

My eyes adjust to the dark, and I see him. Zach is staring at me. He must have seen me walk in.

I close my eyes and take in a deep breath, then make my way over.

"Hey, beautiful." He grins, and my entire body begins to shake. His smile, those full lips. A little less magnetism would help me right about now. As it is, I want to launch myself at him. *Gah!*

This is worse than before we slept together. *I can't do it.*

Oh God, I have to do it. We're working in the same room all night. *Keep it together, Nessa.*

Zach walks around the blackjack table they've set up especially for the party, and stands next to me. He's in a white blazer with a blue crew underneath, his hair spiked for maximum *Miami Vice* effect. But here's what I see: strong forearms where he rolled the sleeves up, shoulder muscles straining beneath the fabric, and dark eyes sparkling back at me.

His smile makes my insides gooey. He could be wearing nothing and still cause my heart to race. Actually, that's a bad example, because Zach in nothing is more stimulating. The point is, it's just him. There's always been something I can't define that draws me to him. And now that I know what that mouth and those hands can do, and how his body feels above mine—I'm a wreck.

Chew, chew, chew.

Zach frowns. He raises his palm. "Spit it out."

My jaw freezes, and I stare at him like he's crazy. "My gum? Into your hand?"

"Do it, Nessa. I'm not kidding around."

I lean over and spit out the gum like he says, my mouth twisting in annoyance. We had better not be back to him treating me like a child.

He balls up the gum in a napkin from my tray, and hook-dunks it into the trash bin behind the bar a few feet away. "Now, what the hell is going on?"

When I don't answer—because how am I supposed to answer that when I don't know?—he grabs my arm lightly and pulls me to the side. "Why'd you leave this morning?" His voice is low, slightly husky, and it does funny things to my belly.

"I didn't want things to be awkward."

"Why would they be awkward?"

"How about because we slept together?" I whisper loudly.

He grins at first, then frowns. "Exactly. It was awesome, so why would things be weird?"

He really needs me to spell this out? "Because we're friends. And you don't have girlfriends, just girls you sleep with. Those one-nighters you're so fond of."

He looks at me pointedly. "With other girls. Not with you."

I stare at him, trying to read his expression. My heart wants to believe he's saying something deeper, but logic says no. "So you're saying you want a repeat?"

His jaw shifts tensely. "I'm saying there's no repeat about it, there's just us. I thought you understood last night that we'd be in this thing once we took the next step. I was trying to spare you by keeping my distance all these months, but you made it impossible."

I look away, incredulous. Why would he be sparing me anything? I've wanted him. He knows that. And anyway... "So it's my fault last night happened?"

I might have thrown myself at him, but damned if I'm taking all the blame.

His brow furrows, as if he's confused. "Well, not your fault, but you know—I told you I was weak where you're concerned." At the look on my face, he adds, "I want more with you. I tried to see you today to talk about it." He glances over his shoulder as a busboy slams a plastic tub of glasses on the counter, then lowers his voice. "I missed you when you weren't there this morning. I went to see you, but you weren't home either, and you didn't return my calls. Why didn't you return my calls?" A desperate edge tinges his tone.

He can't be saying what I think he's saying. That he's serious about having a relationship. I mean, that's what I want, but I need to be smart here. No jumping to conclusions where Zach is concerned, because if I'm wrong, it would break my heart. "Things are different with us."

"Exactly."

"I didn't want you to feel trapped. I worried that you—uh, kissed me, and other stuff—because you felt bad."

Zach blinks several times, staring at my face as if I'm some kind of puzzle he can't figure out. "You're kidding, right?"

"No!" I lower my voice. "No—you've been pretty obvious about not wanting to get involved with me. I got naked. I thought you might have done—well, what we did—out of pity."

His mouth twitches as if he's holding back a smile.

"This isn't funny, Zach."

"No, it's not." He leans in and pecks me on the lips. "It's cute."

I growl. "You know I don't like those nicknames. I'm not cute just because I'm short. And I'm not your little sister."

He cringes and shakes his head. "Dude, no." He leans closer, touching the small of my back with his fingertips. "You are sexy, and beautiful, and I wish we weren't working so we could return to my bed. Or your bed. Either works."

A shiver runs down my spine, my heart rate increasing with his words. I might also be breathing heavily. "Are you sure that's what you want? You're not just saying that because you feel sorry for me?"

His eyes widen. "Nessa, you really want me to show you how I feel? Here?"

"No." I shake my head jerkily. Considering the look he's sending me, which is the exact same look he had last night in the hot tub before he carried me away, we need to steer this conversation in another direction.

But I smile. I can't help it. I'm so happy I was wrong—or that my instincts were right. Whatever. I'm glad what we have isn't like his past hookups. It's not a hookup at all.

Zach grins and kisses my cheek, his lips lingering for a moment. "Later. After work?"

"Yes."

And that's how the rest of the night goes. Hot, sexy looks from Zach, my heart racing, my mind distracted as I hand off cosmos to the guys with the Flock of Seagulls hair, and Sierra Nevada pints to the girls with headbands and Madonna moles. I've sent the wrong drinks out twice now, my tips shot to hell, and I couldn't care less.

At the end of our shift, Zach walks over as I'm cashing out with the bartender. "Can I come over in a little bit?" he asks. "I'd like to go home and shower first, but after? Would that be okay? Not too late?"

It's midnight, but who's keeping track? "Nope, not too late."

"I'll be quick, then. We can grab a bite at the Last Stop."

I watch him stride away. The club is still hopping, because this place doesn't close for a couple more hours. It's dark and seedy, as usual, but my grin is bright. Several people stare at me like I'm crazy as I make my way to the exit a few minutes later.

And I am. So crazy in love.

Chapter Six

Inspired by the Bitchin' Eighties party, I grab a sparkly off-the-shoulder top and pair it with cuffed boyfriend jeans and my platform tennis shoes. Heels would look better, but my baby toe still hurts like crazy.

My heart is racing, and I'm a shaky mess. I'm so nervous about my date with Zach, which is just nuts, because I know this guy. We've been good friends for over a year, but this evening—him coming to pick me up, which he's done a thousand times before—is different. It means something—to me, anyway—and I'm praying it means something to Zach too.

I swipe on lipstick and a knock sounds at the front door. One last glance in the mirror, in which I fluff up my hair, frown, pluck a loose thread from my top, then close my eyes and spin around. There's no use trying to be perfect. He either likes me enough or he doesn't, and no amount of primping is going to change that.

I fumble with the lock and open the door.

"Hey," Zach says, his eyes skimming my body. "You look beautiful."

I let out the breath I've been holding, until I notice how stiff his shoulders are. He seems nervous too, and I can't help but feel wrecked all over again. How can we have a normal relationship? Are we crazy for thinking this could work?

"You ready?" he asks.

"Yeah, let me grab my purse."

Zach walks behind me as we exit. I reach around him to lock the door, and sense him watching my every move. And that has me fumbling the keys when I'm not normally unco-ordinated.

Zach drives to the Last Stop, a local bar/restaurant everyone goes to for after-hours food. Our conversation on the way there is almost nonexistent because of all the tension in the air.

We order our meals and Zach's gaze lands on my hands. He reaches across, touching the thin gold bangles on my wrist, then scoops up my fingers in his.

It's an easy gesture. A normal date thing to do. But Zach and I aren't simply two people going out on our first date. Somehow his holding my hand feels natural—this boy who's never touched me unless he was razzing me. The press of his hand isn't playful, it's loverlike, sending warmth to my chest and face.

"Tell me about your family. Your parents," he says, still studying my fingers, which appear childlike inside his.

Um, okay. He's never asked about my family before. "You already know my dad was born and raised in the Philippines. My mom is originally from Cornwall."

"How did they meet? What are they like? I don't even know if you have siblings."

He doesn't say it in an accusatory manner, but there's a part of me that takes offense. "You've never asked."

His eyes catch mine. "I know."

Was it intentional? I stare at his blunt fingernails, the wide surface of his masculine hand. Intentional or not, he's asking now.

"My dad came to the US on a scholarship to study engineering at Cal Poly. He was taking courses over the summer when my mom and a friend walked into a coffee shop where he was studying. My mom was in the States on holiday, and she and her friend were on their way to Santa Barbara." I smile. "Could be a load of crap, but he said he knew the moment he saw her that he was going to marry her."

Zach is silent for a moment, seemingly deep in thought. "So that's it? He saw her and they got married?"

I laugh. "Hell no. My mom thought he was crazy. He tried to buy her coffee and she turned him down. In a desperate attempt to see her again, he invited her and her friend to a party that night. Technically, he *called* his friends afterward and told them to throw a party because he needed to impress a beautiful girl. My mom ended up going, though."

"And your dad wore her down?"

"Nope."

"Damn. I'm beginning to feel sorry for your dad."

"Not all guys have it so easy."

He frowns. "It's never been easy, Nessa."

I ignore the implication in his tone, because I don't understand it. Zach has dated so many women that I couldn't begin to count the number. I don't get why he held back for so long when it came to me. Or why, all of a sudden, he's open to more. But I'm not going to question it, because being with him is what I want above all else. I don't want to jinx it.

"Nothing exciting happened at the party, but my mom agreed to give my dad her mailing address at her job in London. He wrote to her, called her, pretty much worked his way into her life. Eventually he went and visited her. Supposedly, on that visit she let him kiss her." I shiver. So not cool to think of one's parents hooking up.

"And?"

I roll my eyes. "Apparently she liked it. By the time my mom returned to the States for another visit, my dad had bought a ring and asked her to marry him."

Our waitress sets food in front of us, and Zach takes a bite of the fries that came with his steak sandwich. "That's kind of romantic."

I hide my eyes and focus on my own plate. "I know."

The story of how my parents met is difficult to live up to. Neither my sisters nor I have had much luck in the relationship department. At the moment, we're all single, even my older sister, who's approaching the quarter-century mark. She is, in fact, the most single out of the lot of us. I can't imagine her loosening up enough to let a guy in. I don't even remember the last time she went on a date.

"How'd your parents end up in the Bay Area?"

"My mom hated her job in London, so she moved to California after they married and while my dad finished up his degree. When he graduated, an aerospace firm on the peninsula recruited him. The rest is history."

Zach's brow furrows. "So your dad's pretty smart, then —the scholarship, working in aerospace?"

"Yeah, but he's also down to earth. That's how he wooed my mom and her family. He's a good-looking guy too —I'm the only one who's vertically challenged in my family."

"Any brothers or sisters?"

I forget the extent to which our past conversations have veered away from anything personal. It seems strange that Zach wouldn't know about my sisters, considering how much time I've spent with him, but that could be as much my fault as it is his. He's never asked, and I've never brought it up. We talk about our mutual friends, the things we're up to, work, but never our families. And never the people we're dating—or not dating, in my case.

The only reason I know Zach's mom suffered a tragedy is because I've overheard him talking to his friends about it. I'm also aware that he's an only child. And now he's shared with me his dad's gambling career. But until now, he's known next to nothing about my family.

"I have two sisters. And before you ask, yes, they drive me crazy," I say. He grins. "My older sister is in the Philippines visiting family. She's been there for a few months and won't return for a couple more. We're probably the least alike. She is super anal, and our personalities clash. She doesn't approve of anything I do, and I think she needs to remove the rod up her ass."

Zach laughs. "Man, it's good to be an only child. But for real, it sounds kind of cool to have a sister you clash with."

I give him an incredulous look that only makes him laugh harder. I shake my head and continue. "My younger sister and I are close. She's been living on the East Coast, attending college. I'm trying to convince her to move to Tahoe for the summer when she graduates in a few weeks."

His expression is serious as he says, "That's pretty cool that you have sisters. I never knew."

"You never asked, or seemed interested."

Zach swallows and glances away. "I've always cared. I was just—trying to keep things neutral."

"Why is that?"

He props his elbow on the table and absently plays with the salt and pepper shakers. "You're beautiful, sweet—look at the family you come from. My family is... well, you know."

"I know a little. But Zach, I don't care about your family. I care about you. I like *you*."

He gives me a quick smile. "Cutie—and don't give me grief about the nickname. It's how I see you. Sweet, beautiful girl. Only, I enjoy imagining you with your clothes off too." A naughty closed-mouth grin twists his full lips.

Cutie isn't so bad when he puts it in that context. "I can live with that."

We dig into our food, and I know from experience that Zach can't talk while he's wolfing down his meal. So I wait until he slows his pace, and then I lay it on him—the question I've wanted to ask but never have.

"What happened to your mom, Zach?"

His eyes dart to the side. He sips his water and wipes his mouth. "My mom fell and hit her head several years ago. She never recovered." He looks up, searching my face, but I'm watching him, waiting for more. "She was out with my dad and some friends. It was my junior year of high school. She'd been drinking. I wouldn't call my mom an alcoholic, because she realized she was drinking too much at one point and toned it down. But the night of the accident she drank too much. They were at a party held by some rich Tahoe nob and his wife. There was a large stone staircase." He stops and takes a deep breath, tossing his napkin on the table as if he's lost his appetite.

"You don't have to talk about it if it's too painful."

"No, it's okay. It's just—it was so senseless, you know? One minute she's a wife and mother, working as an admin for a local dentist, and running circles around me and my dad. And the next..."

I reach across the table and link our fingers, staring at our hands together.

"She fell down the stairs, hit her head, and that was it. Lights out. She didn't die, but she lost everything. My mom has been in a long-term care facility ever since. I visit about once a month, and my dad does too, but there's not much point. She isn't on ventilators or anything, she's just"—he shakes his head—"not there anymore."

"What does that mean?"

"Her brain swelled after she fell. She was in a coma for a while. When she woke, she was almost entirely unresponsive. She's been in rehab for years, but there's been little improvement. The doctors say her brain is permanently damaged. She blinks, does all the autonomic things like swallowing, but she needs to be fed, because although she can lift her hands, she doesn't have the motor skills to hold a fork. She doesn't recognize faces. She doesn't know I'm there."

The urge to reach across the table and hug him overwhelms me, but I hold myself back. This is our first date and I don't want to overstep, which is laughable given what we did last night, but there it is.

Overnight, Zach lost his mother. He may be able to see her, touch her, but she's gone to him. My mom is the rock in our family. I can't imagine losing her so young, or not having my sisters to lean on, annoying as they can be. "I'm sorry, Zach. I shouldn't have asked."

"No." He looks up. "I want you to know. I miss my mom, but it's been a long time since the accident. I'm one of the lucky ones. I had a good parent. I'm grateful to have had her for as long as I did."

I don't understand how he can call himself lucky. It sounds tragic. But I think what he's saying is that it could be worse. Mira's drug-addicted mother comes to mind. That's something that can ruin a person, but Mira is resilient. She's grown from the experiences she's had. Zach is resilient too; he just doesn't give himself enough credit.

"Well, I think your mom raised a good son."

He stares into my eyes. "I'm no good, Nessa."

"Why would you say that?"

"Because it's true. That woman you saw me with? The one you asked about?" He drops my hand and rubs his fingers over his mouth. "You were right. It was a fucked-up situation, and it went on for too long. I'm not seeing her anymore, but what I did—holding on to a relationship I knew was wrong—it was messed up."

The pit of my stomach sinks. It's what I surmised, seeing them together, but to have my fears confirmed? Zach has been with many women, but this lady may have been the most constant in his adult life. How will that affect him moving forward?

"Is it really over?"

"Yes. And that has nothing to do with you. Well, maybe a little, but it's been something I've planned to end for a long time. I haven't wanted to rock the boat, but now I don't give a shit."

"Are you—seeing anyone else?"

"No."

"So it's just me?"

"Absolutely." He scrubs his jaw. "You're not, you know, dating that Sal character?" I shake my head. "Good, that's good."

"Is it? Is this really what you want, Zach?"

He huffs out a chuckle. "I don't deserve you, but yeah,

it's what I want." He leans across the table and kisses me lightly on the lips. Not only does it send a zing down my spine, but I also feel like the luckiest, happiest girl alive.

The waitress hands Zach the bill and he pays it, not letting me even get the tip. We drive back to my place and he walks me to the door.

"Do you want to come in?" I ask. It's ridiculously late, but I don't want to say good night just yet.

He runs his thumb along my jaw, his fingers dropping to trace the hickey he left on my neck. His eyes sparkle for a moment, but then his expression sobers. "I should get going."

"Are you sure?" I smile, and if there's a hint of suggestiveness in it, that can't be helped. I'm thinking about last night and how much I want him. He's so close, but for some reason, he still seems so out of reach.

"Yeah." His eyes are intense, staring at my lips. He grabs my hand and drags me to his chest. "But tomorrow—see if you can get off early? I want to take you on a real date."

My heart pounds so hard I wonder if he can feel it through his shirt, which would be embarrassing. "This wasn't a real date?"

He kisses the corner of my mouth, teasing me. "Hmm, it was, but I want an official one. A date where I ask you out in advance. You deserve the best, Nessa, and I want to give that to you."

I lean back and look him in the eyes, trying to gauge what's going on inside his guy head. "I'm not perfect, Zach. You should know this by now. I don't cook well, I chew gum like a baseball player, and I'm short—though I *am* concentrated awesome."

He smiles. "You're perfect to me."

Chapter Seven

Zach

Leaving Nessa on her doorstep last night tested all of my self-control. Everything inside me clamored to throw her over my shoulder, charge into her bedroom, and repeat what we'd done the night before. I held myself back by a hair, and managed to turn my ass around and walk to my truck. Alone.

Tonight there'll be no holding back. Tonight, I want to show Nessa how much she means to me, and how serious I am about her.

I talked another dealer into covering the second half of my shift so I can get off early. I'll have to pull a double to make it up, but it's worth it. Nessa deserves a nice restaurant, not one of the cheap diners that are open all night. I could put off our date until we both have a day off, but the last thing I want to do is wait. I can't explain it, but I need to reassure myself that this thing between us is real. I'm out of my league, no idea what I'm doing, but Nessa deserves the best I have to give.

Blue is packed, a sea of bodies swarming the casino floor, yet I still catch sight of my dad weaving his way toward my table. He doesn't walk with an entourage like the other whales, but the man has presence. And he knows half the workers in the joint, greeting people with a broad smile and a pat on the back as he crosses the floor.

Dad sits at my table and tosses a barney on the felt. "Zach." He nods in greeting.

I shake my head. I hate playing against him, especially when he's wasting half a grand on the house. Stresses me out. I have my own cash now, but I can't help worrying about my dad and his "luck."

"What's up?"

"Just making the rounds."

"How was Reno?"

He flashes a predatory smile. "Profitable."

At least he won in Reno.

"Saw Alexis on my way in."

My hands freeze for a split second, until I snap the fuck out of it and deal the next hand. "Oh yeah?" I say with as little emotion as I can manage. I would be happy to never see Alexis again, but there's no chance of that with her affinity for the table.

"Said she's got a new protector."

I glance up. "Protector?"

My dad signals for another card. I deal it and tend to the other players.

"Alexis has her own money, but she likes to live off of"—he coughs, glancing at the others at the table, who don't seem to be paying attention—"the men she spends time with."

My dad and Alexis run in the same circles, what with

their mutual love of gaming. He would know more about her life than I do. I was just the plaything.

I knew Alexis had other men on the side. Rich, powerful men who gave her things. She sure as hell didn't have the cash she does now back when she was married and hung out with my parents during my high school years.

"You still spend time with her ex-husband?" Jim was a good guy. My impression—now that I'm older and world-wearier—is that Alexis worked him over.

"I see him from time to time. See Alexis more. Jim doesn't have the cash to play the tables that Alexis does. She's a character, that one. Was there the night..."

My dad's face turns strained, pale—this from a man who is perpetually tanned. "The night what?" I prod.

He clears his throat. "The night your mom fell."

I'm not sure what my dad's love life is like these days. I'd rather not know, but I've never seen him with another woman. He loved my mom, end of story.

I clear the cards. House wins and my dad is out a barney. For him, to gain and lose thousands in a night is nothing.

"Mom and Alexis were best friends. I'm not surprised you guys were hanging out the night it happened," I say.

My dad's eyes skim the new cards I dealt face up. "She was the last person to talk to your mother."

I blink, registering his words. I'd always assumed my dad was the last person to talk to my mom.

The pit boss taps me on the shoulder. "Everything okay?" He looks at my dad. "How are you doing, Mr. Elliott?"

My dad and the pit boss chat it up, while I pull myself together and deal cards to the players who hit this round.

"I never knew that," I tell my dad once the pit boss moves on.

"Yeah, well, what's done is done. Nothing we can do about it now, it's the cards we've been dealt." I roll my eyes at his pun. "Always wondered, though, what happened between your mother and Alexis. Your mom was real upset that night."

"You were there. Don't you know?"

He shrugs. "They were in some kind of catfight. Jim and I were smoking cigars. I figured the ladies would work it out. Now I wish—I wish I'd intervened. Your mom hit the bottle hard that night, angry about something Alexis had said."

My mind is racing. I'm thinking back to when Alexis and I began our affair. As soon as I turned fifteen she started flirting with me, touching my arm when no one was looking, hugging me a little too long when she said hello.

That was before my mom fell and became a vegetable.

My dad doesn't second-guess his decisions. "Dad, why are you bringing this up after all these years?"

He doesn't say anything at first. He studies his hand while I wait an eternity for him to answer. "I've seen the way Alexis looks at you. I just want what's best for my son. I've been in a bad place since your mom fell. I'm slowly coming out of it. Some things are clearer. Just want to see you happy, that's all."

I thought no one knew about Alexis and me. Turns out I underestimated my dad's powers of observation again.

My dad plays a few more hands, then stands, stretching his back. "All right, Zach, I'm taking off. Not a winning night for me. I'll see you in a couple of weeks?"

"Sure. You planning on coming through again?"

"I've got a thing in Arizona. I'll be back after that."

"Arizona?"

"Your old man's got lady friends too, you know." He pulls his shoulders square, his expression a bit sheepish.

No, I didn't know. This is a new development.

"How's *your* friend?" he asks. "The one who left you the other morning?"

Of course he'd bring up Nessa's deserting me. My dad may have an unconventional job, but he's traditional in some ways. My refusal to settle down with a girl—*ever*—has been a point of contention. He's rubbing it in that one of them finally stood me up. Not that it's what happened. Nessa running out was a matter of miscommunication. She thought I'd treat our relationship like any other hookup, and that's not the case.

"Taking her out tonight," I say, a little too smugly.

"Good." He pats me on the shoulder. "See you around, son."

I track my father's progress toward the exit as he says his farewells to waitresses, bartenders, a few dealers. Then I wait while the hours pass by more slowly than they ever have in my entire life. I can't get out of here fast enough.

I texted Nessa earlier to make sure we're still on for this evening. She said she had one thing to do with Mira, then she'd be ready. We're meeting up after work, and I cannot wait to get my hands on her.

I held off last night, trying to be a gentleman—who would have thought, right? But tonight—tonight I'm not holding back. Time to make sure Nessa and I are on the same page about this thing we have going on. And if I have my way, she'll know she's mine and I'm hers.

The thought makes me so damn proud.

What do you know? For the first time in a while—or ever, for me—both Elliott men have someone special in their lives.

Chapter Eight

Nessa

Zach has run home to take a shower after work, and it gives me just enough time to meet with Mira. While I requested to get off early for the night, Mira and a few other executives are working late because of a party the casino is hosting for a pro basketball team. Mira suggested I go upstairs to meet the lady in charge of the internship, since she's working late as well.

Mira is trying to sell me on the unpaid position, which is really unnecessary. I will work for free if it gives me a foot in the door in the management department of Blue Casino. Mira makes bank in the executive offices, and she loves her job. I'd take an unpaid internship in a heartbeat, just as long as I could fit in my waitressing hours; a girl's gotta put food on the table.

I change out of my uniform and into a sleeveless, stretchy beige dress that hits mid-thigh and complements my dark hair. I pair it with nude platforms and a lightweight denim jacket. The shoes are more platform than heel. Pinky toe is feeling better and the swelling is gone, but I'm not ready to brave stilettos just yet.

I wonder what Zach would think if he knew I'd fallen on my ass in an effort to escape his room the morning after. That was one hell of a walk of shame. Then again, the way he'd put me in the friend zone all these months, I was convinced he'd wake and think it a mistake.

I've never been so happy to be wrong.

Hmm, maybe if I tell Zach the story, he'll give my pinky toe a kiss and make it feel all better? Or kisses in other places?

Okay, time to get my mind off the boy I'm dating —*dating!*—for at least the next thirty minutes while I meet with Mira and the manager.

Mira's at her desk when I enter her office, her heels kicked off and tucked to the side as she pounds away on her keyboard.

"Knock, knock," I say.

Her face brightens and she shoves her keyboard under the desk. "Yay, you made it just in time. Deborah's about to leave."

"Are you sure this is okay? I don't need special treatment. I'm happy to apply like everyone else."

"Well, yeah. You'll have to apply. This is just a little early intro." Mira stands and slips on her shoes, straightening her skirt. "Deborah's going to love you."

"And you want to give me a leg up on the competition."

"*Totally.*" She hugs me with a Machiavellian grin.

"You're bad, Mira."

"No, just assertive. And aggressive. Those are good traits, right? Anyway, Deborah is a marketing guru and super forward thinking. She's going to be so excited about the social marketing you did in college. Plus, very few people who apply for internships have worked on the floor. You're already ahead of the game."

We walk down the hall, and Mira introduces me to Deborah, talking up my experience in e-marketing. Just like Mira said, Deborah seems interested in the internships I completed in college. The casino is moving away from direct mailings and into Internet marketing, so it seems like a good fit.

By the time Mira and I leave Deborah's office, I'm even more optimistic about the internship. I'd planned for a position like this when I graduated from college—paid, of course. Minor detail. Working at Blue on their marketing team would be the perfect opportunity to gain experience with a national employer.

"Well, that went well," Mira says, her eyes bright with excitement. "I would be surprised if you didn't get the job. You have the experience they're looking for and you work here, so they know you're reliable."

"I don't want to get my hopes up." Which seems like something I've been telling myself a lot lately. Considering how well things have worked out with Zach, maybe I should be more confident.

Mira wraps her arm around my shoulder and squeezes so hard my neck cracks. "Gah!"

"Sorry, I'm just so excited. We need more girl power around here. This place is overrun with domineering men."

Blue's management team doesn't have the best reputation, but most people think it's gotten better since they fired the guy who caused all the trouble last year.

She glances down the hallway. "How much time do you have? Can you spare a few minutes to check out one more thing? I want to show you the coolest place in the casino."

Her nose scrunches. "Not sure I'm supposed to bring people in there—"

"Oh my God. Don't do something that's going to get you in trouble."

She waves me off. "Nah, you have to see the security room. It's right here, and the guys in there love me."

I roll my eyes and smile. "Of course they do. I can check it out, but just for a sec. I'm meeting up with Zach soon."

Mira pushes open a heavy double door and we step inside. The air crackles in this room, the walls and desk surfaces filled with electronic equipment. It even smells like computers—heated plastic and new carpet.

"Wow." I look around. "This *is* cool."

Several men and one woman sit in front of dozens of tiny monitors tracking every aspect of the casino floors.

"Come on," Mira says. "We'll make a quick sweep."

She walks me around the room, and I peer at the gaming floor and parts of the casino I've never seen from this stealthy new vantage point. My gaze stops on one of the small monitors, and I look more closely.

Mira backtracks and looks at what has my attention in a death grip. "Is that...?"

"Zach," I say, prickles of unease running up my spine.

What's he doing on one of the hotel floors? Zach said he was running home after work. He's picking me up at Blue, but we're supposed to meet in the casino bar.

I don't want to keep watching, but it's like a train wreck about to happen. I can't look away.

Zach knocks on a door, and a woman answers. The same blonde he said he wasn't seeing anymore. The woman grins and throws her arms around his neck, kissing him on the mouth in a not at all friendly way.

My breath hitches, my stomach roiling.

Zach pushes the woman inside the room, and the door slams shut behind them.

Nooo. Why would he...?

Mira shakes her head. "Zach. So typical." She studies my face. "Hey, you okay?"

I swallow, but nothing comes out. No sound, no air.

"Nessa."

"Can we leave?" I choke.

We walk into the hallway, and Mira stops me with a light hand on my shoulder. "What's wrong, Ness?"

"I don't feel well."

She scans my face. "Give me a minute. I'm about to take off too. I can give you a ride. The security room is always so hot with all the monitors, and computers, and... Are you sure you're not going to pass out?"

"No. I'm—"

Not fine. Sick at the heart.

I grab Mira and press my face to her shoulder, holding back the tears, but it's no use. They come out anyway.

"Nessa? Oh my gosh. Come on." She drags me to her office. I wait while she shuts down her computer and collects her things.

Mira doesn't ask me what's wrong, but she looks at me every few seconds as she drives me home, as though she thinks I'm going to die or something. I can't blame her. I feel like I'm dying.

I didn't bring my car to work. Teresa drove me in, since I was planning on going out with Zach...

Tears run down my cheeks, my chin. I'm not a badass who can keep it all in. My face and body have always betrayed my emotions. To make matters worse, I'm a sloppy crier, my face hot and likely blotchy.

I wipe the tears with the sleeve of my denim jacket.

Why would Zach do this? I don't understand. He dated around, sure, but he's never been a jerk. He doesn't lie to people. Not to me, or any other woman that I know of. From what he and his friends have said, he's always been direct about his intentions and inability to commit. When he told me he wanted more, and asked me out tonight, I thought... I *believed* him. Believed I meant more to him.

But he lied when he said things were over between him and that woman.

Mira pulls up to the cabin she and Tyler share. Tyler's at his computer when we walk in, but he stops what he's doing and stands to give Mira a sweet kiss. He looks over at me, and his eyebrows pull together. He whispers something to Mira, and she shakes her head. The next thing I know, Tyler's climbing the ladder to their loft and Mira is shoving sweatpants and a sweatshirt at me.

"Put these on," she says.

I stare at the clothes in my hands. "I should go home."

"Nope. You're staying with me. We're having a girls' night."

Sometimes it's easier to do what Mira says than to argue, and right now I don't have the strength. I put on the clothes.

Mira changes as well, and brings out a bag of chips and some sodas. "This is the only trashy food in the house at the moment." She tugs on my sleeve until I sit beside her on the couch. "Now tell me—what's up, Nessa? And don't say it's nothing. Something is definitely wrong. Was it the surveillance room? *Zach?* You seemed to change the moment we saw him enter that woman's suite. That didn't bother you, did it? Have you guys..."

"No." I thought we were more, but I was stupid to think it.

Nothing has changed between Zach and me. And there's no reason to mention how foolish I was to think otherwise. I already feel like an ass.

My phone buzzes in my purse, vibrating the couch. I reach over and pull it out of my bag. It's a missed call from Zach.

The phone vibrates again, but this time it's an incoming call. He's calling me back.

I stand and walk toward the back door, stepping outside. "Hello?"

"Ness, where are you? I thought you'd be off by now. You still with Mira?"

"Yeah."

"Okay, well, how much more time do you think you need? Should I go ahead and order you a drink?"

"Where were you tonight, Zach?"

"What do you mean? I was working."

"After work. Where did you go?" I sound like a nagging wife, pushing him for answers, but I need to hear him say it.

"I went home to change. Nessa, what's up? You sound upset."

"What did you do once you returned to the casino?"

Silence—then, "I waited around for you."

"You didn't visit anyone?"

"What are you getting at?" His tone is deep and serious.

"I saw you with her. The woman you said you weren't seeing anymore."

He sighs. "How did you—never mind. It's not what you think."

"We can't be friends anymore, Zach."

"*What?* Nessa, this is crazy. Give me a chance to explain."

"Did you kiss her tonight?"

"Fuck, that's not how it happened."

"Did you or did you not put your mouth to hers and shove her in the room?"

"I—yes, but it wasn't like that."

"Goodbye, Zach." I end the call and turn my phone off so I won't be tempted to answer it again.

I don't understand why he's been stringing me along and acting like he wanted something serious. Had I given him the idea I'd be okay with him dating other woman while we saw each other? All's fair during a hookup, but I made sure he wasn't seeing anyone before I agreed to go out with him.

Why did I think things would be different between us? Zach never has girlfriends. I should have known something like this would happen. But I'd waited for him for so long. I wanted the chance to prove we had something special.

How wrong could I be?

I breathe in the cool evening air and sit on the step to the patio. Mira and Tyler's backyard has no landscaping, just a square concrete slab. The rest is native trees, dirt, and pine needles.

I've always liked their backyard. It's pure. True. Unlike the boy I love.

I'm finished pining for Zach. He's not capable of anything more than cheap encounters. Though what we shared didn't feel cheap. It felt real.

I tuck my knees beneath my chin and cover my head with my arms, tears spilling down my face. My head and heart have never been more conflicted.

Chapter Nine

Zach

I knew my relationship with Alexis would bite me in the ass one day. I couldn't be involved in something so wrong without the universe paying me back. Now that it's hurt my chances with Nessa, I wish my dumb fifteen-year-old ass had said no to Alexis when she first started coming on to me.

I storm out of the casino. It's my fault. I should never have responded to that note Alexis had someone deliver. The only reason I went to her room was because of my dad's comments earlier. I wanted to know what happened the night my mother was irrevocably changed.

Alexis had lied to me. Well, not lied. Omitted. She has never once told me she was there the night my mother fell.

I knocked on the door to her suite, intent on getting answers, but before I knew it, her arms were around me, her mouth plastered to mine.

In the middle of the damn hallway.

I shoved her inside the room. "What are you doing?"

"You came," she said. "I knew you couldn't stay away for long."

Running a hand through my hair, I sighed in frustration. "I thought I made it clear, Alexis. I'm not interested in a relationship with you anymore."

"Oh, really? Then why did you come? Stop fighting this, Zach. We'll always be in each other's lives. You'll always be my lover."

How had I never noticed her stalker tendencies? The woman was losing it.

I should have left right then, but I came for answers. "What happened the night my mom fell? Why were you two arguing?"

Alexis's eyes darted to the side. "What are you talking about?"

"My dad said you and Mom were in some kind of fight, and that's why she drank so much. Did you have something to do with her accident?" I moved toward her. "And don't even think about lying. I'll know if you are."

Alexis might be a miserable person, but she isn't a good liar. Her fingers are her tell. She'd twist a loose string, the hem of her top—whatever was at hand. It's why she never played poker. She couldn't bluff.

Her eyes widened. "No. I swear. I had nothing to do with her fall."

"Then why was my mom upset that night?"

Her gaze darted to the side again, as if she was nervous. "She didn't like how close you and I had become. She didn't understand us, Zach."

My shoulders suddenly felt like cement blocks. "So it's my fault my mom got hurt."

Alexis grabbed my arm. "It's not your fault. It was no

one's fault. Your mother tripped at the top of the stairs. She fell and landed wrong. We were arguing that night, but she was my friend. I never wanted anything to happen to her. I didn't push her, if that's what you're worried about. I was at the bottom of the landing."

I shook off Alexis's hand and walked to the picture window overlooking the lake that held some of the clearest water in the world. Amazing that I could look at something so beautiful and be surrounded by such ugliness. Alexis might not have pushed my mom down the stairs, but what she and I were doing had caused my mom pain —and those had been her last coherent thoughts.

I sensed Alexis approach from behind. "What we have is special. Your mom didn't get it."

"What we had was filthy," I said over my shoulder, then turned to face her. "I want nothing to do with you. So help me, Alexis, if you come anywhere near me again— my place of business, my home—I'll go to the police and tell them you raped me when I was sixteen."

"Ridiculous. You wanted it."

"Did I? I was a kid mourning the loss of my mother. I was vulnerable and you took advantage. The only reason I haven't gone to the police before now is because I felt partially responsible, but I won't let that stop me anymore. And if you think you're going to turn around and try your hand at another underage kid, think again. If you come near me or my girlfriend, or if I hear even a whisper about you and some kid, I'll press charges and show proof. Consider this your warning."

"What proof?"

I gave her a look.

"Those emails? If you still have them, that just proves how much you wanted what we shared. And there have

never been any other young men—as young as you were,"
she clarified. "You were special. You are special."

"You're sick, Alexis. Get help. And don't forget my
warning. You know I don't gamble. I'm not bluffing."

"Zach!" Alexis called as I strode to the door. I shot her
a glare, and her expression fell. She cradled her chest, her
lips pressed together. "You'll come back to me, and I'll be
waiting."

"No, Alexis, I won't." I left and never looked back.

As soon as I was out of the hotel elevator, I attempted to track down Nessa on the casino floor. No one had seen her for over an hour. I waited a little longer, then called—and discovered Nessa knew all about Alexis and the kiss in the hallway.

She fucking *knew*. How did she know?

Didn't matter. I'd just ruined the best thing that'd ever happened to me.

* * *

Nessa

I scrub at the dried tears on my face. It's been almost half an hour since I got off the phone with Zach, and Mira hasn't come out searching for me, thank God. She's giving me space.

Maybe Zach had a good reason for meeting with that woman tonight, but what kind of reason could he have for kissing her?

I'm so tired of being in love with him and not having my feelings returned. He doesn't see me the way I see him, and it's time I gave up thinking things can be different. The night we spent together was one of the best nights of my life —but I need to lock it in a box and forget about it.

My stomach clenches. I press on the ache one last time before rising. I take a deep breath, tuck my hair behind my ear, and open the back door to the living room.

Mira's on the couch studying me as I walk inside. "Ness…" she says, her face a silent question.

"Is it okay if we don't talk about it right now?"

I don't think I can handle spilling the story about how naive I've been thinking Zach really cared about me.

She nods, and I sit next to her. She turns on the television and we watch a reality show. No idea which one. My brain is numb, while my body switches between pain and nausea.

A knock sounds at the front door, and Mira looks at me.

I shake my head. "It's not for me," I say, staring blindly at the television screen.

Mira stands and opens the door. Zach is there. He's wearing dark jeans and a button-down shirt with the sleeves rolled to his elbows. He looks handsome, but his eyes are tense and worried.

His presence steals my breath. My entire body hums with anticipation.

Damn my body.

How can I go from aching pain to fluttery anticipation in the span of a heartbeat? I feel everything when he's near. I always have.

I want to run and hide.

I want to press my face to his chest and have him wrap his arms around me.

I am a conflicted mess.

Zach remains just beyond the threshold. "Nessa, can I talk to you?"

Mira walks to the center of the room. "I'll just—" She looks left, then right, but her and Tyler's place is miniscule. The single bedroom is right by the living room, and the walls are thin. There's nowhere she can go that would give us privacy.

"Will you come for a drive with me?" Zach asks.

I nod. I don't think it's a good idea for me to be alone with him. I don't want to be talked into something my heart is too freaking weak to fight. Where Zach is concerned, I want my head in charge for once, and maintaining distance is critical. But he's right. There's no place for us to air our dirty laundry without both Mira and Tyler hearing.

I grab my purse and slip on the nude heels I wore to Mira's. I'm still in borrowed sweatpants and a sweatshirt, but whatever. Zach has seen me in worse. Or in nothing at all. *God.*

He presses his hand to the small of my back and walks me to his truck, opening the door for me. It's such a boyfriend move, and it pisses me off. He's not helping to resolve the confusion between my brain and my heart.

"I'm sorry, Ness," he says once we're on the main road. "I should have told you what happened with Alexis. I thought I could ignore it, that it wouldn't affect us, but I was wrong. I don't want to hide anything from you." He glances at me, and damn my heart, it beats faster.

My brain is firing all sorts of lovey-dovey messages at the sincere look in his eyes. Which means I'm in trouble. Brain and heart can't be on the same page if I'm to put an end to what can only be a painful, one-sided relationship.

"There's nothing you can say that will make me change my mind, Zach. Even if it was just a kiss, you told me it was over with that woman, and it clearly isn't." I don't care how much I want to be with him, I won't put up with that crap.

"You don't know the whole story. I pushed her away as soon as we were in her hotel room. I told her—*again*—that it was over."

He lets out a deep sigh. "When I started seeing Alexis, I was young and vulnerable. I take responsibility for getting involved in something I knew wasn't right. That relationship dragged on way too long, but I'm not feeding you a line when I say it's over. For me, it is."

He pulls into a driveway and turns off the engine, and I realize we're in front of his house.

"Nessa—Alexis and anyone else I've been with are a part of my past. I want you to be my future. I don't deserve you, but I want you. What you saw tonight was Alexis not taking no for an answer. I've convinced her she needs to. And if she doesn't, I'll go to the police because I'm tired of her crap."

"What are you talking about?"

"The only reason I went to Alexis's room earlier was to get answers about my mom's accident. I'd just learned that she'd been there when my mom fell. But Alexis did what she always does and took advantage of the situation. I've known her most of my life, and I never want to see her again. That's the truth."

He pushes out a sigh. "From the moment you and I kissed, Ness, I considered you mine. I've always considered you mine. Almost planted a facer on that Sal guy for trying to date you."

"That's not what Sal—"

"Yes, it was. Trust me, I know how guys think. And if any man has even a fraction of the feelings I do for you, he'd be trying to lock it in. I know that doesn't make sense, considering I never did anything about my feelings, but no matter what, you've had my heart. I was just too afraid of fucking things up to do anything about it. I wasted a lot of time, but I love you, Nessa. I've been in love with you for a long time. You're the most beautiful person in my life. Please—Christ"—he tilts his head back in anguish—"please give us another chance."

I'm not happy he waited so long. Not happy about this Alexis woman trying to cling to him. But for once, my head and heart are in perfect agreement.

I reach for him, and he grabs my waist and pulls me close, hugging me as tight as he can despite the armrest between us.

He kisses my face, the lids of my eyes. "I'm sorry, I should have told you sooner what happened tonight. Should have told you everything. Just didn't want to lose you."

I pull back. "You keep saying you don't deserve me, but you deserve happiness, Zach, even if it's with someone else. But I'm happy you chose me." I smile, and he kisses me deep and handsy, just the way I like it with him.

"I'll always choose you," he murmurs between kisses.

"I love you too, but crappers, you made me wait a long time to be together."

I feel his face break into a smile against my neck. "You can punish me, beginning now. Just as long as we're together."

He raises his head and kisses me until I can't breathe. I don't even want to. Who needs oxygen for your brain when your heart has known all along what was right? Should never have doubted my heart.

My heart is a genius.

Chapter Ten

Deborah, the marketing manager at Blue Casino, along with Hayden, Mira's boss, and Adam Cade, some executive from hospitality, sit behind a long table interviewing me for the marketing internship. I'd be nervous as hell too, if this interview wasn't so entertaining.

"So, Nessa," Hayden says. "You indicate in your résumé that you were in charge of social media for the university during your last year of college. Is that correct?" I nod, and she turns her back to Adam, her body angled toward Deborah. "Deborah and I have spoken about finding someone to help with the social media accounts. It's a large job. That alone could take up the internship."

"I'm used to social media. I had a system for keeping up with it for the university. I think I could handle it and still have time for other projects."

Adam sits forward and leans his forearms on the table, nudging Hayden in the side and forcing her to scoot over. "Hospitality will be working closely with the marketing department this year. Efficiency with social media is key if the intern is to attend meetings and help facilitate communication between the two departments."

Hayden's mouth compresses. "Adam, this intern will not be answering to hospitality. Even if he or she did, they wouldn't answer to you."

Adam's lips twitch. "Of course, Hayden. You're the boss."

Hayden's eyes narrow on him.

Deborah glances at the two of them, then gives a subtle eye roll. "Adam makes a good point. At the pace our business runs, an intern who could help bridge the communication gap between departments would be an asset."

Hayden squares her shoulders, bumping into Adam's arm. But instead of moving and giving her space, he leans into her, his leg brushing against hers under the table.

Hayden's face turns red.

The executives are so much more entertaining than the floor employees. This is like watching my smut television.

"Well, I think we have the information we need," Deborah says, cutting into their nonverbal battle.

Hayden asks if I have any other questions, then wraps up the interview.

"How did it go?" Mira says when I walk into her office a few minutes later.

"I think it went well." I raise my eyebrows, my face pulling into a wide grin.

"That's an awfully cheerful look on your face. Was it that good?"

Now that Zach and I have been officially dating for the last couple of weeks, and there's no more tension or uncertainty between us, it's easy to laugh and find the humor in life.

I silently close the door and sit in the chair across from

her desk. "The interview went really well, but—what's the deal with Hayden and Adam?"

"Oh God, were they fighting?"

"Something like that. I'm not complaining, though, because watching them kept me from being nervous."

Mira shakes her head. "They need to bone down already, but it's taboo because she's his boss and he's got this stick up his ass, which leaves them—" She holds her fingers up in fake claws and makes a growling sound.

"*Wow.*"

Mira shrugs. "Exactly. They're killing me. I'm trying to stay out of the line of fire."

A light rap sounds at the door, and Hayden walks in a second later.

"Oh, hello, Nessa. I came to see Mira, but I'm glad you're still here. Do you have a minute?"

"Of course." I stand, wondering if I should offer her my seat. It's the only other chair besides Mira's. I settle for standing nervously.

"Well," she says with a smile, "I spoke with my colleagues and—you got the internship. It was unanimous. We're very excited to have you on board. In fact, Adam and Deborah are rather anxious for you to start. We're back-logged up here and could use someone with your abilities."

"Oh my gosh, *thank you.* And yes, lay it on me. I can start as soon you want."

She grins. "Excellent. I'll give you a call this week to discuss schedules. I understand you're still working at Blue as a waitress. There shouldn't be a problem working around your shift if you think you can commit three to four hours in the afternoon?"

"Yes, no problem."

Adam walks past the doorway, and I swear Hayden's

back straightens. As if she senses him, she glances over her shoulder, then smiles stiffly at us. "Wonderful. I'll be in touch." She walks off in the opposite direction.

Mira heads to the door and closes it behind her boss. "Oh my God, oh my God!"

"I got it," I squeal, my cheeks cramping, I'm smiling so hard.

* * *

Zach

I don't know why I'm nervous. I wasn't the one with the job interview. But that's my girl at Blue, sitting across from the bigwigs. I don't want her to get hurt.

See—this is why I was afraid to take a risk with Nessa. I want to protect the hell out of her. And love her. Love her in my bed too, because damn, that's fun. My mind drifts to last night and the position we pulled off in the hot tub. Gotta do that one again. Soon. The hot tub has become my new favorite place to spend time with Nessa.

I shake my head. All I do is think of my girl.

My girl. I like the ring of that. She's mine and I'm hers and that's all there is. I grin as I prepare the chicken for tacos tonight. Everyone's coming over for our weekly dinner. No more sick girlfriends holding the boys back, and no work obligations. I have it on good authority that there are no Blue events tonight, so Mira has no reason to flake. Even Tyler wrapped up his book edits and will be here.

The whole gang is back together. It'll be the first time we've hung out since Nessa and I became a couple.

Some of the guys have asked me what's going on. They suspect things, especially after I picked up Nessa from Mira and Tyler's place and never returned her. Never heard the end of that one from Mira. And while I don't care who knows that Nessa and I are together, I don't feel the need to go into details about how it came to be. Nessa's the most important person to me. That's all they need to know.

The door creaks open and I spin around. Nessa plops her purse on one of the living room chairs and walks over, giving me a big hug. "Mmm, you feel good," she says.

She knows I'm dying to know what happened. She's totally leaving me hanging, sassy little thing. I grab her ass. "Well? How'd it go?"

She reaches around and steals shredded cheese from the counter, stuffing it in her mouth. I watch as she chews, a wet, pink tongue swiping a small piece off her plump bottom lip.

I haul her closer. "You had better give me the abbreviated version, because watching you eat—it's giving me ideas. We've got business to take care of before our friends arrive." I waggle my eyebrows.

She reaches down and palms my erection. "I got it."

My mind draws a blank. "Got it?" My erection. Yes, yes she does. I lean down and kiss the smooth skin of her neck. "What, babe? Me? Yup, but you already know that."

She starts unfastening the row of buttons at the top of her white blouse, which is tucked into a narrow brown skirt that accentuates her beautiful curves. I pull out the hem of her top and work on her lower buttons.

"The internship," she says.

I slide the shirt down her arms and toss it aside. "You got it?" She grins, and I squeeze her in a bear hug, careful not to hold her too tightly. My cutie is petite and I don't want to hurt her. "Congratulations. Not that I doubted it. Of course you got the job. Who wouldn't want you?"

She grins and leans toward my ear. "Now, where were we?" she whispers, and I feel her pulling my shirt up my back.

I jerk it over my head and quickly kick off my pants. I remove some belt thing she has cinched around her waist that's probably the height of fashion, but looks like a samurai sash to me, and shove up her skirt, then lift her in my arms.

"Our friends will be here in half an hour, but you deserve lots of pleasuring for doing such a good job today, so we better hurry."

She giggles and wraps her sexy legs around my waist as I run with her down the hallway to my bedroom. I leap and twist in midair, landing backward on the bed, Nessa on top.

"Ahhh!" she cries above me, her body bouncing—all the good parts, anyway.

I drag her mouth down and kiss her while my hand slides up her leg to the sweet spot I've been thinking about all afternoon. Damn, my girl is hot.

Nessa sits up and shimmies out of her panties, her skirt hiked around her waist. She tugs at my boxers. I lift my hips with her on top so she can get them down far enough. Cool air hits my erection, and then her soft, warm body covers me.

I groan. The perfection of her body against mine is something I will never get over. We fit together—we always have. In every possible way. I was just too afraid to reach for it.

As I consider the ways in which I love and want to love Nessa, my heart rate kicks up and pressure builds in my groin. As turned on as she makes me, this could be over in two minutes if I'm not careful—okay, one, if I'm being honest—but that's not gonna happen.

I flip her over and inch down her body, unfastening the pretty lavender bra she hid, the bad girl, underneath her business top. I kiss one breast, then the other, my palms following the path of my mouth. I unbutton her skirt, consider taking it off, then decide it's too much work and I've got places to be.

My eyes linger on her pretty legs and the part of her I consider my personal heaven. Holding the backs of her thighs, I push her legs up and lick her center.

She moans. I do it again and again, enjoying the little sounds she's making, but it's not enough. I want her out of her mind.

I insert a finger and find the spot I discovered the other day that she really likes.

Her breath hitches. "Zach," she says, her voice breathy and sexy as hell.

I don't stop. My mouth, my hands, are all over her, pleasuring and loving her until she cries out, her body convulsing, hands clamping a pillow over her face.

She tosses the pillow aside and blows a lock of hair out of her mouth. "Agaah... Can't talk."

I kiss the inside of her leg and inch back up her body. "No need. Just let me do the work."

A wicked glint shines in her eye and she sits up, straddling my lap. Before I can figure out what position she's going for, I'm inside her and she's falling on me, my legs pinned beneath us. This might end in a hell of a leg cramp, but I'd rather lose a limb than stop.

I grab her ass and kiss the beautiful breasts that are bobbing in front of my face—the sexiest sight imaginable. As predicted, my release comes hard and fast, and if I'm not mistaken, she comes too, because I feel her milking me for everything I'm worth. And you know what? She can have it all. I want to give her everything and more.

Our breaths are uneven as I straighten my legs beneath us, Nessa still straddling me and nestled in my lap.

I roll to the side and take her with me.

She turns over and I spoon her from behind. I could easily pass out.

Nessa reaches back and slaps my ass. "No sleeping. They'll be here soon." She climbs out of bed, her cute little butt swishing on her way to the bathroom.

"Where are you going?" I croak.

"To shower, Zach. For real, you can't fall asleep. You're the one who feeds us."

True; none of my friends can cookt. Gotta fix that. Putting a crimp in the alone time with my girl.

I may want to pass out, may not feel like getting up and feeding my friends, but you know what? It's a good problem to have.

Nessa is my blue streak in the sky—that flash of lightning that knocked me off my feet when I first met her. I never thought I deserved her, but I do. I've finally grabbed on to her bright light, and there's nothing better than sharing my life with her. Because I'm the guy who's going to care for her and love her more than any man has ever loved a woman. I may piss her off from time to time, but I'm never going to give her a reason to doubt my devotion.

She has it—all of me.

Epilogue

Zach

I pull up to the small, brown, run-down dwelling near Nessa's old apartment. Two front doors face the street, a pitched carport in the center separating the two units. "Well? What do you think?"

"It's—" Nessa cocks her head, taking it in from another angle.

"A piece of crap," I say for her. "But I'm going to fix it up. Don't you think it has potential? With new paint and a little landscaping?"

So far, Alexis hasn't tried to reach out to me since she kissed me in her hotel room, and I haven't seen her at the casino. I think she's finally taking me seriously, thank God. I don't want to go to the police, but I will if she tries anything again. Now that I have Nessa, I just want to continue to build what we have together. Nothing's ever felt more right.

Nessa smiles at me. "It's awesome. And I'll help. We'll make remodeling it a project. In fact, I bet the gang will help too."

Now, there's an idea. About time my food-freeloading friends lifted a hand. They've been using my kitchen as their own for years. "I'll call them this afternoon. Escrow closes in two weeks, and if we plan it right, we can get in and make the upgrades quickly. The faster I get the work done, the sooner I can get renters in."

I have dreams of owning a few duplexes and making a living off the rent. That's a little ways away, but this is a start. Owning land gives me the stability I crave, and working at Blue with Nessa while I build my empire means more time with her.

Blue is about to hire Nessa as a full-time employee in the marketing department. She's only been there a few months, but she's kicking ass so hard, they've already moved her from an intern to a part-time employee.

"Lewis has all that extra gravel lying around in his yard, now that his landscaping is finished," Nessa says. "I wonder if he'd let you have the rest? Oh my gosh, and you could get Jaeger to make cute wooden shutters with pine trees cut into them. It's going to be so adorable! We could even have a painting party."

I grab her and kiss her firmly on the mouth. "A topless painting party?"

"With our friends around?"

"Dude, no. Before our friends come. Like a topless prep-party for the painting party—one that involves just you and me. Exactly the way I like it."

I haven't said anything to Nessa, because I don't want to scare her away, but the fire under my ass to own more property is because I want to be able provide for us. If Nessa wants to work, I fully support her. But I want to be able to take care of her no matter the situation. That's important to me.

She shakes her head in exasperation, but there's a naughty grin on her face. "Topless-hot-tubbing-after-the-painting party?"

"Sold."

* * *

Dear Reader,

I hope you enjoyed Nessa and Zach's story in *Never Date Your Best Friend*!

Are you ready to find out how Hayden will whip the bad boys of Blue Casino into shape in the final installment of the Never Date series? Or maybe you're just curious about Hayden's sexy new colleague, Adam, and his role in Blue's old boys' club?

Grab ***Never Date Your Enemy***, the final book in the Never Date series!

xoxo,
Jules

Never Date Your Enemy

Adam Cade is entitled, arrogant—and he doesn't remember me.

Adam is the prince of Lake Tahoe, born into one of the wealthiest families in the area, and he's the one person I hoped to avoid.

He doesn't recognize me.

He definitely doesn't remember how he helped this town ruin my life.

Now that we work together, I have no choice but to get close to the arrogant ass if I want to keep my job.

Only the closer I get, the less I see of the guy who wronged me in high school, and more of the sweet, sexy man he is now.

EXCERPT

He stalks across the room, his hair combed, his suit couture, in typical Adam fashion, and not at all like the casual man I glimpsed over the weekend. But the dark intent in his eyes is exactly what I saw beneath that polished exterior.

The same eyes that made me mad with lust this morning.

***Never Date Your Enemy* is an enemies-to-lovers romance with loads of sexy banter and a meaty plot that will keep your eyes glued to the page. Grab it now!**

Grab *Never Date Your Enemy* Now!

Also by Jules Barnard
USA Today Bestselling Author

All's Fair

Landlord Wars

Roommate Wars

Never Date Series

Never Date Your Brother's Best Friend (Book 1)

Never Date A Player (Book 2)

Never Date Your Ex (Book 3)

Never Date Your Best Friend (Book 4)

Never Date Your Enemy (Book 5)

Cade Brothers Series

Tempting Levi (Book 1)

Daring Wes (Book 2)

Seducing Bran (Book 3)

Reforming Hunt (Book 4)

About the Author

Jules Barnard is a *USA Today* bestselling author of romantic comedy and romantic fantasy. Her romantic comedies include the All's Fair, Never Date, and Cade Brothers series. She also writes romantic fantasy under J. Barnard in the Halven Rising series *Library Journal* calls "...an exciting new fantasy adventure." Whether she's writing about steamy men in Lake Tahoe or a Fae world embedded in a college campus, Jules spins addictive stories filled with heart and humor.

When she isn't in her sweatpants writing and rewarding herself with chocolate, Jules spends her time with her husband and two children in their small hometown in the Pacific Northwest. She credits herself with the ability to read while running on the treadmill or burning dinner.

www.julesbarnardbooks.com

www.ingramcontent.com/pod-product-compliance
Lightning Source LLC
Chambersburg PA
CBHW061548310726
48972CB00008B/2669